KAIKU

By

Roxanne Barbour

Roxanne Barbour

KAIKU – Roxanne Barbour

Cover Artist: Steven Novak

Chapter One

everyone involved
uncovering
treasures and adventures

The mound moved, and I fell.

Not down the rabbit hole, but close enough. Our exploration group had stopped to lunch on the flat top of a smidgen of a bump in the ground cover. Standing too close to the mound's edge when the earth shuddered, I lost my footing and tumbled down the small hill—landing on my rear. A few of our group of humans and Keeki scrambled down to come to my rescue. Trying to get my embarrassed body upright, I braced my left arm on the side of the mound. However, I soon found my arm buried in the dirt.

"What *are* you doing, Cadet Carter?" asked Major Sylone Craig, the human leader of the Earth Sciences Force's expedition on the planet Needles. Why didn't she just use my full name, Cadet Mileena Charlotte Carter, to embarrass me further?

"Just trying to stand," I replied. What did she think I was doing?

"Actually, I want to know why your arm has disappeared." A hint of a smile played across her slim face. Taller than I, at about six feet, she exuded authority—a necessary attribute with this bright group of exploration personnel.

And my superior loved teasing me. Just because I was the youngest member of the human contingent didn't mean I shouldn't be taken seriously. After all, a doctorate in exobiology at sixteen made me proud. However, Sylone was always available for conversation and advice, so I decided not to obsess about her teasing.

Tyne Tone, one of the Keeki cadet counterparts on our team, grabbed my right arm and pulled me up. I shook him off. Sometimes annoying, the Keeki were strong compared to most humans and, on average, taller and thicker in body. I suspected their evolution from birds, including their vestigial wings, contributed to their physique.

"Why is there an opening in the side of the hill?" asked Major Craig.

Not a hill, in my opinion. Actually, not much more than an eruption of soil, really. However, I did understand her gist about an opening—otherwise my arm wouldn't have passed through the thin surface. "I did notice my wandering hand touching a smooth object. Maybe a rock is buried inside?" I asked.

"*everyone involved,*
uncovering,
treasures and adventures," said Tyne.

The Keeki habit of uttering what sounded like haiku made me name their version of English, *kaiku.*

"Not a bad suggestion, Cadet Tone," said Major Craig, and then she raised her voice. "Okay. Let's finish lunch everyone, and then we can pull out our excavating tools." Sylone had grasped the Keeki *kaiku* soon after they'd joined our crew. The rest of us took a bit longer.

Someone grabbed my pack from the top of the mound while I found a flat spot at the base. No way was I clambering up any mounds again—at least not today.

I ate my lunch while I ruminated on this strange planet, and my bruised and shaky body.

My nemesis, the mound, stared at me. Although shorter than my initial impression, I was actually glad of its diminished height—any taller and I'd possibly have broken a bone on my descent.

Bland light green-brown vegetation covered all six mounds. Nothing remarkable, but at least some greenery. So far, we'd discovered little plant life on Needles.

My glance wandered to Major Craig. She certainly did cut a striking figure. Her short brown hair added to her regal stance, and her piercing gray eyes added to her elegance.

I found Tyne sitting a few feet away from me. Although the Keeki were stocky and muscled, Tyne's own six foot height gave his body a veneer of grace. The faint blue scales on his skin also upped my interest. I decided to spend time getting to know him better. Our expedition had only recently begun, so contact had been minimal so far.

Nourishment helped my body regain its equilibrium, so my thoughts turned again to Needles.

With little greenery and low rolling hills, in some ways this planet challenged my comfort level. My home town of Vancouver was one of the sweet spots of Canada. Surrounded by mountains—ski hills mostly—lush valley vegetation, the Pacific Ocean, and a West Coast rain forest climate, Greater Vancouver had everything. Of course, a parochial viewpoint, but this planet radiated dullness in a majority of its aspects.

Needles had one thing going for it, though—every once in a while color splashed our eyes.

The glorious sunsets decked out in red and orange intrigued me and, although the planet had little thriving low level ground vegetation, wondrous trees existed. The shapes and colors astounded me. Each small grove contained numerous tree types. From thin trunks to stout ones, from tiny trees to tall ones, each grouping contained many varieties, much to my surprise.

Each tree leaf encountered had a variegated green-orange pattern, but numerous leaf designs were evident. The shapes of their leaves tended towards round.

As for why we'd called this planet Needles, we blamed the Keeki. They'd wanted us to join them in an expedition to study this planet new to both of us. In support of our new diplomatic relations, Earth agreed. However, we'd had no idea what to expect. Hence *Needle in a Haystack* became our motto.

"Time to start digging," announced the major, after most of us had finished our lunches. "Let's do a proper dig; you all know how."

Before leaving Earth, the members of the expedition had been trained, or retrained, in archaeological digs. Human and Keeki alike.

So we staked and took pictures and videos before we began to remove the hillside's surface. Not long later, the major made us cease our digging. She reached into the hole my arm discovered and pulled out a chest with a green lid and gold trim. The rest of the artifact was a dark brown.

Although smudged with dirt, the artifact exuded warmness—perhaps because of its rough and glistening surface. What would make a chest twinkle? Gems? Unusual chemistry? Or maybe, alien DNA coated the surface? Perhaps an exobiologist needed to pursue my question, and that would be me. I smiled to myself, and my curiosity kicked in. After receiving a doctorate in exobiology, my interest in other worlds propelled me to the Earth Sciences Force's

Academy. And, after two years of academic courses, I was now on a training mission—a practicum, by any other name.

"Okay, everyone, let's sit down and we'll discuss how to proceed. And then I'll assign today's duties," said Major Craig, pointing to a flat spot a short distance away. She needed to temper our enthusiasms with reality. Not that enthusiasm was a bad reaction in an exploration group.

Most of the group turned and followed her, but I lingered. The chest drew me in; it resonated with my left hand, for some strange reason. Perhaps my initial contact had created a harmony, an understanding of some sort.

Without thinking, I reached out and touched the artifact. After a momentary hesitation, the lid rose, and my curiosity made me peer inside.

****

After I opened my eyes, the first thing I saw was Briny's face. "Why are you here? I thought you stayed back at the ship for testing?"

"You're a little confused, Mile," said our resident medic and scientist. Her blue eyes sparkled, and she gave a little toss of her tied back long blond hair. "You lost consciousness at the dig, so Tyne picked you up and ran back to base. Your crew hadn't travelled very far today so it didn't take him long to get here."

I tried to sit up, but Briny gently pushed me back down. "Just rest. Whatever gas you exposed inside the artifact knocked you unconscious."

"I'm poisoned?" I asked. I did a mental check, but my body didn't feel too bad.

"Probably not, but I've taken blood samples, just in case. I'll know soon enough."

I caught the look on her face. "Actually, you may not. Who knows what alien bug or chemical is running around Needles, ready to attack us? Remember, I'm an exobiologist." All the possibilities flooded my mind.

"A little paranoid, sweety." Briny smiled and rubbed my shoulder. "Rest a while. Major Craig and the crew should be back any moment," she said, taking my blood pressure. "It shouldn't take them long to pack up and bring the rover back."

A good friend of mine now, Briny and I had clicked on the trip out, and spent hours discussing alien physiology—of which we both knew little—but our ignorance hadn't stopped us from speculating.

Then I remembered my situation. Aack! Major Craig! I tried not to think about her response. I dozed as weird objects swirled in my mind—images of misshapen mounds and strange shaped treasures.

"Sleeping on the job are you?" asked Sylone, interrupting my dreams.

Apparently, the crew had returned. "Ah, ah, sorry. Tired for some reason," I said. My gassing had affected me far more than I'd realized. I sat up and looked around the small infirmary on our landed spaceship. Because there was only enough space for Briny, Sylone, and me in the room, a bunch of heads peered through the doorway.

"Briny, would you mind leaving for a few moments?" asked Major Craig. "And slide the door shut behind you, please."

She smiled and shooed everyone away so Sylone and I had privacy.

Not sure if I welcomed this time alone with our leader, I said nothing.

"Not too bright, Cadet Mileena Charlotte Carter," Major Craig announced. With her arms crossed, she glared at me.

"I know, I know. I have no idea what happened. I'm normally more responsible. Somehow the artifact put me in a trance, and I didn't comprehend my actions. I'm sorry; it won't happen again, Mom." Embarrassed, I decided to stop talking.

"I'll have to put some sort of notation about this incident on your service record, you know. Just don't do anything like that again." Sylone stepped closer and gave me a non-regulation hug. I hugged her tightly in return. "Now, have a cleanup, since you probably feel grungy after your ordeal, and then join the crew in the break room. We're going to have a meeting."

As a youngster being dragged along with my mother on her various Earth Sciences Force's exploits, I'd developed a taste for travel, and the time had allowed my home study education to proceed at a fast rate. When she'd recently spent two years at Earth Headquarters, my chance to speed through my university education and start at the Earth Sciences Force's Academy had happened. With two years of study at ESF—and now time for my practicum—the

ESF authorities had reluctantly allowed me to accompany Mom on her current expedition. Family members weren't usually allowed together but, because of my youth, they'd made an exception. To my current knowledge, on our expedition our relationship was only known to Briny, our medic.

On the way to my room, I ran into Tyne. "Thanks for carrying me back. I hope I wasn't too heavy." His build certainly indicated strength. Again the faint blue scales on his skin stood out.

"*emergency plan,*
escaping,
base medical welcome," Tyne replied.

What did Tyne try to tell me? The Keeki followed an emergency plan unknown to me?

"*lightness of body,*
burdenless,
aroma, touch, unusual," he continued.

Again, what was Tyne trying to say? He didn't like my smell? He didn't like how I felt when he carried me? Looking on the bright side, apparently I was no heavyweight.

Although I'd read through the mission documents, and listened to all the briefings, I now realized my negligence in researching our journey companions. I needed to study the Keeki. Time to remedy the situation.

"Well, I'm going to freshen up; I'll see you at our meeting." Walking past him, I gave a quick glance backwards. He'd also turned toward me, so I pretended to straighten my clothing. My glance revealed tufts of what I could only call peacock hair. Thinking back, I realized all Keeki, male and female, sported spiky, shiny, blue and green hair.

And, much to my surprise, I detected a whiff of a pleasing but unusual scent. A cross between rosemary and sage, I decided.

What would I have noticed if I'd been conscious when Tyne carried me back to the ship?

I was the last to arrive to our combination galley/meeting room. A couple of crew members snickered, but I ignored them and sat beside Briny.

"Okay, let's start," said Major Craig, getting everyone's attention. "It's time to plan our next moves regarding the artifact."

"Keep Mile away," a low voice mumbled.

Major Craig sent a glare to her left, but I had no idea who'd spoken.

"We're going to study the artifact Mile discovered. Cam, Briny, the artifact's in your science lab. Take an hour to do some surface testing. We've taken pictures and video recordings already, so scan the surface and take samples. I don't think you're going to find much, but you never know. Then we're going to open it up," said Sylone.

I slunk further down in my chair.

"Everyone else, update your daily reports—either here or in your room. We'll regroup in the lab in an hour."

I scurried to my room for privacy. Because of my eventful day, the time allotted made updating my report a challenge.

****

After the whole human/Keeki exploration group trickled into the lab, Major Craig took charge. "Cam, Briny, all tests complete?"

"Yes," replied Camothy Beal, our lead scientist. With two decades of ESF experience, he exuded confidence. And his short, slightly graying brown hair, slight build, and calm demeanor, helped his image. "Briny and I found nothing unusual. A little Needles dirt and such; nothing we wouldn't have expected from a box buried in a hillside."

Major Craig, said, "Okay, stand back everyone. Cam, put on your face mask, who knows what's still left inside. Open it up, please, and be careful."

Things he would've done anyway, but he tactfully tolerated Major Craig's orders.

Cam turned on the lab's exhaust fans and found his mask. The rest of us backed up a few steps. The artifact resided in a windowed enclosed chamber, with the attached exhaust fans on full suction.

Opening the chest proved anti-climactic. Because of the fans, nothing could be heard or smelled, so we used our eyes.

The outside consisted of rough stone with hints of gold, green, and brown. The inside contained four chambers. "Do we need further tests, Major Craig, or can we just dig in?" I asked. A couple of laughs wandered my way. My reputation had been damaged with my recklessness today, and my comment wasn't particularly astute.

"Cam, take pictures, and then let's set the contents out on four separate tables. We'll also need samples from the insides of the chambers."

So we idly chatted while Cam took additional pictures, and then we emptied the four chambers. Actually only three—the fourth contained nothing.

"Cam, Briny, see if you can determine anything unusual from the empty chamber; any chemical characteristics, unusual textures, fibers, and such," said Major Craig. "Tyne, you work with Squid on that table; Aran and Mile here; and Mist, you're with me," said Major Craig, pointing at the various piles. Mom split up most of the workload with human/Keeki pairs. The female, Mist, was the other Keeki cadet, and Squid was the second human cadet.

We put on gloves and started our analysis.

I glanced around. Most pairs appeared comfortable with each other, except for Mist. The female Keeki exhibited what I regarded as a sullen facial expression. Did being paired with Major Craig upset her?

Pretty, in a Keeki way, Mist's skin tended toward red, and her elegant posture impressed me. Even her tufts of hair revealed glints of red. Was this a female Keeki trait? For some reason her bearing implied arrogance. Of course, my minimal experience with the Keeki hadn't given me a lot of information to work with.

Time passed while we documented the large artifact and its contents.

Eventually our work was done and we relocated to an empty table in the break room.

"Aran, Mile?" asked Sylone.

Aran Silo, the leader of the Keeki, waved a hand; I assumed he wanted me to do the reporting on our investigation. "The objects we recorded appear to be household items. We found articles like plates and bowls and cutlery. Although we can't be a hundred per cent sure until Cam analyzes a sample, we think the plates and bowls are a kind of heat-processed crockery. Certainly designed to be long lasting. Now, saying these items are plates and bowls is a bit of a leap because we didn't find any remnants of food on them. They're also more square-shaped than I'm used to, but I do think they're dishes. Aran?"

He made a motion with his head; his tufts fluttered. I assumed his head movement meant agreement.

Although Aran was the Keeki leader on this expedition, we'd rarely had a chance to speak. While we'd worked on our section of the artifact, I'd noticed a faint acrid lemon aroma coming from his familiar Keeki slightly blue, gleaming scaled skin. Shorter than Tyne by a couple of inches, he'd appeared timid as we worked together. Not a trait I'd expected from a person in authority.

"Our conclusions came about since the other items in our chamber looked like knives and spoons, and maybe a two-tined fork," I added. "Oh, and they were made from a metal of some sort. At least the cutlery looked like metal."

"Lots of items for further analysis, I see. Tyne and Squid, what did you find?" asked Major Craig.

Squid glanced at Tyne. Getting no response, he said, "We found numerous sealed containers. Since the sides were clear, we got a good look at the insides. The objects appear to contain dead plant life. We didn't open any of them, but we did take loads of pictures. The majority of the contents were orange-brown. I'd expected green-brown, for some reason," said a bemused Squid.

"Just a little human-centric, I imagine," said Sylone. "I'll contact Earth to see if they want us to sample the contents. Although, with Mile's recent reaction, I'm not inclined to open any sealed container."

After the major laughed, everyone glanced my way. I focused on the floor of the break room. Too much attention had come my way today, so I wanted to hide from my immediate world.

Diverting the group's attention, Major Craig said, "Mist and I studied the third partition, and we found what appear to be crystals and rocks. Hard to tell if the crystals were made naturally or in a lab, but I'm guessing nature. And, of course, I'm not even sure if any of the items in the chest are from Needles."

Now that notion surprised me. Why would someone, or something, plant artifacts on Needles?

"Everyone, please complete your reports and send them to me. I will redistribute. When you have time, go back to the lab and take a good at what we've uncovered today—particularly the items you didn't study. Keep your eyes open during our future travels on this planet. Perhaps something will match what we've discovered today."

Sylone sighed. “Okay, let’s have a meal. I don’t know about anyone else but I’m starving.”

I interrupted. “Major Craig, what about the empty section? Why would there be one? Seems strange.”

“Yes, it does. Even stranger that the artifact was so easy to find and uncover,” she replied, glancing at the Keeki.

Mist turned away from Major Craig, and Tyne and Aran locked glances.

“Tyne, what do you know?” I blurted out. Their glances convinced me they hid important information.

Chapter Two

wisdom words
available
unknown race deposited

The Keeki withheld information. Even for aliens their faces implied guilt.

Apparently, Major Craig agreed with my assessment. “Aran, what do you know about these artifacts?”

“*unknown artifacts,*
revealed,
new area uncovered,” he responded.

Analyzing his stark words revealed my lack of understanding of Keeki thought processes. To my mind, he’d contradicted himself with his kaiku, and I wasn’t the only one who’d noticed.

“What’re you saying? Artifacts were revealed to you before? Or you’ve never seen these items before, or they were in a different area?”

Major Craig’s exasperation was obvious to me. Of course, being my mother, I’d experienced her moods previously.

“Yes,” replied Aran.

A single word response, from a being who usually spoke in a bastardized haiku, surprised me.

“Which one of my questions are you answering?” asked Major Craig.

Aran didn’t respond.

“Tyne, Mist, would either of you like to help us out here?”

Numerous glances bounced amongst the Keeki, but neither Tyne nor Mist responded.

Color rose on Sylone’s face. “Okay, since I can’t get a straight answer, the Keeki are now confined to their staterooms when not requiring sustenance. Further exploration, by any Keeki, is also forbidden.”

Major Craig got their attention. Keeki didn't like, *really did not like*, to be confined. Many challenges had surfaced on our trip to Needles.

Mist and Tyne stared at Aran.

"*artifact images,*
viewing,
on home planet," said Aran.

Aran shook his head, and with that motion I believed he'd try to clarify his statement. All humans struggled with the kaiku they uttered.

"*missing items,*
translating,
studied by scientists."

Aran scratched his head while his words twisted our brains. I didn't think his clarification added anything to our understanding.

"*wisdom words,*
available,
unknown race deposited," he continued, after a moment.

Sylone glared. "Are you telling me your own exploring party dug up artifacts, some containing symbols, replaced the cache, tidied up, and then took a portion of the artifacts home to Keeki to be decoded?"

I had no idea how Mom had dug out her question, but Aran gave the Keeki equivalent of a nod of agreement.

"Then contacted Earth with a made up story about exploring a new planet?" continued Major Craig.

Aran again indicated assent with his head movement, I thought. I really needed to go back and study the expedition materials we'd received. What information had I missed?

"Why didn't you explore this planet yourselves?" Mom asked. Indications of her rising temper caught my attention.

"*beacon indicating,*
translations,
return of owners."

Aran made a strange movement with his body. A cringe, perhaps?

"Are these different artifacts from the ones you found previously, and decided not to tell us about?"

This time, Aran's head motion was extremely tentative.

Major Craig paced around the lab. "So, you wanted humans to be here when the aliens returned. Well, that's a fine state of affairs. I want those translations, and I want them now, Aran. Everyone else, eat. I need to send a message to Earth." The major stomped out.

I thought about my mother's anger and, since no ideas about how to deal with the Keeki came to mind, I dug up some nourishment.

Then a thought popped into my mind, so I sat with Tyne, and the human cadet, Squid. "Tyne, why did the Keeki hide this information? Not a very nice thing to do, obviously, and Keeki-human relations are going to be strained because of your actions," I said.

"*Keeki authorities,*
hidden,
cadets not consulted," said Tyne.

"That's a cop-out," said Squid. "When you found out, you could've told us—especially Mile and me."

I objected. "Squid, that's unreasonable. Tyne's a cadet, just like we are. Would you have given a secret away?"

"We wouldn't know any secrets." After he uttered his words, Squid jumped up and walked toward the kitchen area. I'd annoyed him, and not for the first time.

Squid and I had actually gone to the ESF academy at the same time. Earth Sciences Force had a three year program, and I'd been accepted after receiving my doctorate in exobiology. Receiving a similar doctorate, but from a different school, Squid had obtained his at eighteen. A stocky, tall human with red hair and green eyes, no one ever ignored him.

Since entering the academy the same year, we'd taken numerous classes together and got to know each other a bit.

After second year, all cadets were sent on a training mission. Because of our exobiology schooling, and the brand new expedition involving the Keeki, both Squid and I landed on the same mission—with my mother. A bit of a challenge for me and Mom. I had no idea how Squid felt about his current assignment.

Tyne, Squid, and I ate in silence until Major Craig, Aran, and our pilot, Major White, entered the break room.

"Listen up, everyone. I've sent a message to Earth with our extraordinary information. Check your coms; you should've received a copy of the Keeki translation of the records left by this new alien race. After everyone's had a chance to eat, we'll discuss the translations," said Major Craig.

The three of them gathered their dinners. I studied the translation for a while, and then I decided I needed dessert—my mind buzzed after reading the Keeki attempt at English. And the details of my strange and emotionally exhausting day continued to flood my mind.

How did I get into these situations—falling down hills, uncovering artifacts, getting gassed—and now, involved in an alien conspiracy?

And the weirdest recent thought of all, was I perhaps becoming attracted to an alien?

"I imagine you've all had a look at the report I sent," said Sylone, interrupting my thoughts. "Any ideas? Any explanations?" Because the Keeki language structure generally baffled humans, their record translations obviously invited more confusion, and not just by me. Sylone could've asked a Keeki to explain further but I suspected she knew their additional discourse wouldn't necessarily clear up any ambiguities.

Cam jumped in. "I think the translations are saying *we're on our way.*"

His comment unsettled me. Another alien race we needed to deal with? Why hadn't I interpreted the information that way?

"That's also my opinion," replied Major Craig, "but when they'll arrive is the big question. Who knows how far away the owners of this planet are, and when they'd even get the bounce from the beacon the Keeki unearthed?"

"What beacon? How's the message propagating?" I asked. Too many surprises in one day; my heart pounded.

"We believe this chest is actually a transmitting device, and I found an orbiting satellite on further investigation. So if a message was actually sent from this planet, the satellite could've redirected it to the planet's owners. However, we have no way of telling if any messages were broadcast, or where they went," replied Major White, our pilot.

"So what're we going to do?" I asked. "Go back to Earth?" Not an option I really wanted to consider.

"The first thing we're going to do is wait." Major Craig studied our group to determine the mood. Satisfied with whatever she read, she continued, "We're going to wait until Earth responds. I'm sure they'll have an opinion or two about our next actions. In the meantime, we're going to explore Needles. After all, that's why we came here."

Her comments made sense to me, and I did want to see more of this planet. We'd only just begun our explorations. Convinced further delights awaited me, I decided tomorrow couldn't come soon enough.

"We have an early start in the morning, and a really busy day. Plan your evenings accordingly," said our leader.

Anticipating a great day, my excitement grew, so my body wasn't ready for sleep. I watched some people leave, and then I asked, "Anyone want to join me in a game?"

Squid, Tyne, Mist, Cam, and Briny, remained with me in the galley. No one gave any negative indication, so I asked, "I have my game of *Ticket to Ride* in my room. Should I get it?"

"Why not?" said Cam. "We're all travelers."

Cam and I laughed, but the others had no idea what amused us. Obviously, they'd never played *Ticket to Ride*.

"The game's not hard to understand. You start explaining the rules, Cam; I'll be back in a moment." I ran to my room and found my portable copy. Created from thin, strong plastic, the box and contents took little room. Returning to the break room, I found two tables pushed together.

Cam grabbed the game from my hands. "Set it up, Mile. I'll continue my explanation." He rummaged in the box and took a sample of the contents. I put the board out and organized the rest of the playing pieces for everyone. We had the recently reprinted North American version.

"I understand the destination cards. You need to complete the routes across the board—

the ones mentioned on the destination cards—to get points," said Squid. "And to do this you need to collect train cards so you can claim parts of your desired path with your little plastic trains. What I don't understand is why these actions are necessary?"

I laughed. "It's a game—something to give pleasure. Simply put, the player with the most points wins. Points are awarded when you complete a city-to-city route, and additional points are collected at the end of the game when you show your completed destination cards. The game comes to an end when one of the players is down to their last two or fewer little trains. Then all points are added up. Of course, you lose points if you don't complete your routes on your destination cards."

Tyne piped up,

"*winning game,*

exploration,

success or failure."

With no idea what he meant, I guessed. "You're right. This game is like our exploration of this new world—no matter what we find, we're winners. So let's give it a try." A little naïve on my part, perhaps, but Tyne didn't argue with my explanation.

As our game of *Ticket to Ride* progressed, I discovered more about my traveling companions.

Tyne appeared to be trying for the longest routes he could find. Of course, extra points were given at game's end for the longest rail line but I didn't think that was Tyne's reason—I thought he just wanted to explore. I also suspected he had some kind of pattern in mind for his routes, and not because of the destination cards. I felt he enjoyed our game—if only I could read minds.

Cam and Briny, our scientists, approached the game in a logical manner—almost like a computer program—and the game lent itself to their idiosyncrasies.

Mist, I just couldn't figure out. I had no inkling about her approach to the game, and I received no indications as to whether she enjoyed our pursuit.

Squid, on the other hand, made derogatory comments throughout the game. His words touched upon his opinions regarding the simplicity of the rules, the ugly game board, and the silly little trains.

Of course, coming in last didn't improve Squid's mood.

Not a gamer, was our Squid.

While we packed up *Ticket to Ride*, I said, "Anyone have a game they'd like to introduce us to? I'm not ready to turn in just yet."

"*puzzle game,*

teaching,

planning and competing," said Tyne. Then he jumped up and left the break room. The four humans glanced at Mist for an explanation of his kaiku. However, she merely said, "Wait."

Occasionally, the Keeki substituted one word for their normal haiku, which totally freaked me out—I kept waiting for the rest of their words.

In a short time, Tyne returned with paper and writing utensils. He started by drawing a five-by-five grid on a piece of paper, then coloring in some of the squares.

Then he uttered another single word, "Clues."

We watched while he added numbers to each row and column.

Because the Keeki also used base ten, they'd taken them little time to convert to the symbols we used.

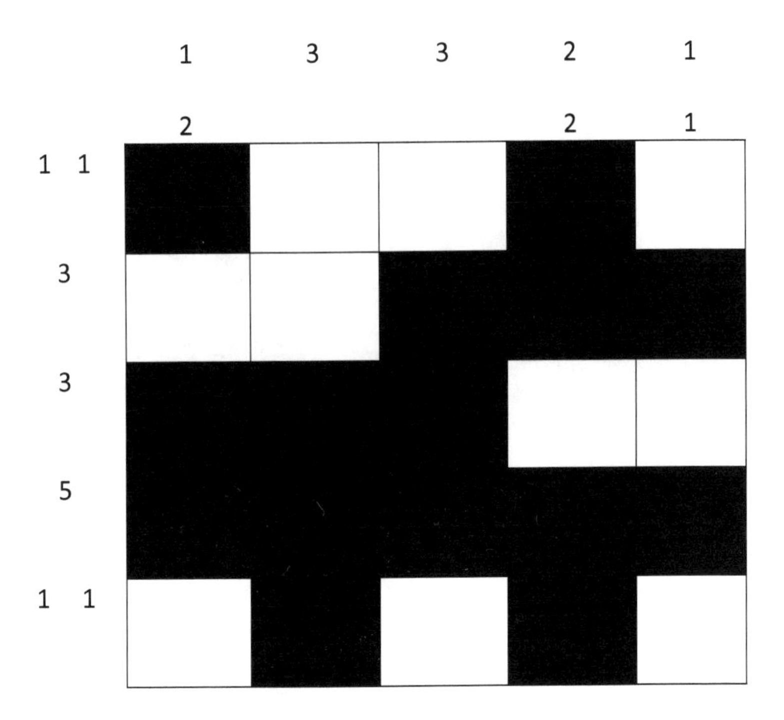

Tyne's puzzle triggered some familiarity, so I entered *grid puzzle* into my com's search engine. Immediately, my screen turned up *griddlers* and *nonograms*.

"I got it," yelled Squid. "Those numbers indicate the patterns of filled in squares for each row and column. This is a great puzzle, Tyne."

Irritated Squid figured out the process before I did, I thought about what my research on nonograms had revealed—there must be at least one blank square between each run of filled-in squares. And look at the bigger numbers first because they have the fewest possibilities on the row or column, so they can be figured out first.

"Okay, my research says, although the patterns of filled in squares can be random, quite often they'll turn out to be a picture. Apparently, you can also do them in various colors." I turned to Tyne. "What do the Keeki call this type of puzzle?"

"*popular game,*
Gyrk,

competitions and fame," said Tyne.

Cam grinned. "This resonates with my mathematical background. I can only imagine the grids getting bigger and bigger. Of course, the bigger they are, the longer they'll take to solve."

A puzzle to solve was one of Cam's happy places.

"Most of the time, a few of the squares are filled in when you start, according to my research. Well, at least for human puzzles. Tyne, this is great! Can you give us an easy one to work on?" I asked.

He held up his hand indicating, apparently, the universal symbol for *wait.* He tapped into his com. In a moment, the printer located in the break room ejected a piece of paper. Tyne stood and went over to the machine and studied his output, and then he printed more copies.

He gave one to each of us, and I studied mine.

"Wonderful. I think I'm going to turn in now, but I suspect I'll be working on this before I sleep. Thanks again, Tyne. I love puzzles."

Our evening ended. Everyone stood and wandered off, one by one. We needed rest before our big day. Since I took the time to gather a bedtime snack, I was the last to leave the break room. I ran into Squid loitering in the hallway.

"You're still here," I commented. His presence surprised me. Usually, he disappeared before everyone else.

"I wanted to see you safely to your room. You've had an exhausting day, passing out and all." Squid rubbed the back of his neck.

Safely? What did he mean? We resided on a spaceship. Did he think space monsters would ooze out of the walls?

Uncertain as to how to respond to his solicitousness, I didn't speak as we walked.

I stopped at my room, which happened to be adjacent to Squid's. "Well, good night. Tomorrow should be interesting."

He reached out a hand and touched my cheek. "Yes. Many sights to see." He turned away and took a couple of steps to his own doorway, and entered his room without a backward glance.

Uncomfortable after his advance, my night turned about to be restless.

Chapter Three

wider circles
three
side by side

Early rising didn't agree with me, at the best of times.

Looking around the breakroom, a number of animated faces were visible, but also a few tired ones. My personal fatigue came from spending too much time last evening working on nonograms, and thinking about Squid. Nonograms delighted me. Regarding Squid, I had no idea how to describe my feelings.

"Listen up, everyone. Working with Major White and Aran, we studied our map of Needles and, of course, the Keeki translations. We came up with four sites to investigate while we wait for Earth's response," said Major Craig.

What about the Keeki response, I wondered?

My com pinged, and a map appeared.

"The first two locations are within a reasonable range for our rover. For the third and fourth sites, we'll move the ship. Our first destination is Mile's favorite; we're going back to the mounds," commented my mother.

A little laughter erupted. "I'm hoping the owners of this planet left other clues in those little hills," said Major Craig. "Or, at least, fairly nearby."

"I have a good feeling Mile will be able to find her vibes again," said Cam, grinning at me.

Much as I liked Cam, he didn't need to add to my embarrassment; I did well enough on my own.

Sylone ignored Cam and said, "Finish your breakfasts, then pack food and beverages for the day. I'd like to put in a full day of exploring." She glanced around the break room. "And, we're leaving in thirty minutes."

Our trip was short since the mounds were only a short distance away. After we assembled outside the rover, Major Craig issued instructions. "Before we start digging, Cam and Briny are going to scan the hillsides for any anomalies, and Mile and Tyne will follow them with metal detectors. After the results are in, the rest of us will map the mounds according to their findings. Hopefully, likely digging spots will become apparent."

Cam and Briny activated their scientific scanners, and Tyne and I turned on the metal detectors brought along in the rover.

We walked closely behind the other two, and all four instruments recorded directly to Majors White and Craig for their analysis.

"Cam, why do you think the mound I was on yesterday shuddered and made me fall down its side?"

"Fate, perhaps?" suggested Cam.

"Seriously?" And he was *seriously* starting to annoy me.

"No, I was trying to be funny," said Cam, with a grin, sensing my mood.

I didn't respond. There was no need to encourage his behavior.

After a moment's silence from me, Cam sighed. "Okay, probably seismic activity of some sort. We've got recorders running full time in the lab. So, if we get any tremors, I'll be sure to let you know, so you can plan your day." Cam laughed.

My annoyance multiplied, but I didn't say a word.

Travelling up and down six mounds consumed a great deal of energy. Thankfully, when we'd finished traipsing, break time had arrived. Grabbing my backpack, I rummaged around for sustenance, and then plunked myself on the ground. Tyne sat beside me and we ate while studying the countryside.

Glancing down, I commented, "The vegetation doesn't seem to have a lot of life, growing life I mean."

"Seasonal?" asked Tyne, his eyes darting about.

"Maybe, but the color of the grass—ground cover I guess would be a better word—doesn't seem to match the color of other plants I've seen on Needles. Appears almost dead," I said, running my hand through the stubby covering.

Other members of our expedition overheard my comments and began looking around our immediate area. "Agreed," said Cam. "However, I think we should wait until we've seen more of the planet. Maybe this area has an unusual soil mixture, or plant life.

Needles is big and should have an abundant variety of vegetation and animal life."

"We have much to learn," commented Sylone. "Mile, why don't you and Squid and Tyne grab your packs and start cruising the area, while the rest of us dig. Take recordings and pictures and be back by dinner time. That'll give you lots of time for exploration. Mile, you're in charge of the away team today."

I loved her idea. The three of us jumped up, grabbed our gear and walked a short distance away from the rest of our expedition. "How are we going to do this?" I asked. "What kind of search pattern should we use?"

"*wider circles,*

three,

side by side," said Tyne.

"Not a bad idea, Tyne," said Squid, "since the mounds we've already discovered are themselves somewhat arranged in a circle."

Circles, with an ever increasing circumference from the mounds' center? I also approved of Tyne's suggestion. So we started walking. Of course, on the first circle round we spent a good portion of our time looking back and watching our fellow explorers on the mounds.

We stopped at our starting point. "Let's summarize what we found, or didn't find," I suggested, enjoying my role as team leader. "Squid?"

"Pretty much the same ground cover as at the mounds. Similar color, same texture as well. Not much else."

"Tyne?" I asked. I wondered what he'd say. Since the Keeki spoke in so many different ways, I hoped to hear a new vocal cadence.

"Similar. Further," he said, pointing away from the mounds.

With little found on our first pass, we needed to expand our search pattern.

So we stepped a good distance away from the first path, and started on our new circular route. First we encountered odd-shaped trees. Their limbs resembled twisted oars pointing to the ground with the yellowish leaves reaching for the sky. Uneasy, the three of us glanced at each other and then back at the trees. According to our instructions, Squid took leaf and bark samples.

"This bark is brittle. Do you think the tree is dead?" asked Squid.

"*life lacking,*

unhappy,
sight of sadness," said Tyne.

Startled, Squid and I studied Tyne. How could a tree be unhappy? Had we uncovered a life form? Did Tyne know something we didn't? Had the Keeki hidden further information?

"Why?" I asked. "Why is the tree unhappy?" Weird to be uttering such a question. Did Keeki trees have intelligence? Is that why Tyne thought this Needles tree had a problem?

"Sustenance lacking," he replied.

Okay, that answered one of my questions—Tyne thought the tree lacked nutrient. I still didn't understand, though, how he came to his conclusion.

"Make sure you include the information in your report. Okay, guys, let's move on." There wasn't anything else we could do at this point.

Emerging from the grove of trees, we found markings disturbing the ground cover. Actually it seemed more like something had eaten the surface away in various places. After photographing and taking samples of our find, we sat under a tree and took a break.

"These grooves on the ground are interesting," I said. "Does anyone see a pattern?" I certainly didn't. As mysterious as crop circles, their significance eluded us.

"Maybe it's a message; something we need to decode," suggested Squid. "Or maybe it's a puzzle. Tyne, have the Keeki seen these markings before? I mean when the Keeki were previously here."

"*limited expedition,*
searching,
until first discovery."

Tyne gulped liquid from his pack like he was in a desert. Come to think of it, the area was awfully dry.

By his kaiku, I gathered he meant the original expedition had proceeded only as far as discovering our group of mounds, and then high-tailed it for home. As risk takers, humans would've probably explored a larger portion of the planet before returning. By now, we recognized reasons why the Keeki asked for our assistance.

"Third circle," said Tyne, pointing even further away from the original mounds.

Time to get moving. We could probably manage one more longer circuit, before we needed to return to the rover.

A short distance past the ground markings, we came upon today's motherlode. Four new mounds—similar in height to the first ones, fifty percent wider, and flatter on top—sat along the edge of a pond.

"Let's circle each mound and take pictures and videos. We need to look for signs of another cache," I said. The better part of an hour elapsed while we performed our duties. Covered in vegetation similar to the first hills we'd encountered, nothing new caught our eyes. A couple of likely cache spots appeared but we didn't touch anything. I, for one, didn't want to be devoured again.

After we finished our documentation, we picked up our bags and wandered over to the pond. The opposite side was visible, so we unanimously decided to take a stroll along the shore line.

The pond water shone in the weak Needles sunlight. No action marred the glistening blue-mauve surface. Did the pond contain any marine life? Hard to tell. but we took water samples anyway.

Eventually, I sat on the shore to rest and think. The guys sat a short distance away. Apparently they'd recognized I needed a bit of private time.

My right hand rummaged in the sand while I gazed at the far shoreline. What shall we call this lake? Maybe it could be named after one of us—the great discoverers. An egotistical thought, I decided.

My thumb found a lump in the sand. The shore sand turned out to be filled with pebbles—a few translucent with colored strands, others solid colors. "Guys, can you help me find more of these pebbles? I need a sample I can study." I showed Tyne and Squid my discovery.

"Sure, but first I'm going to take a big sample of the sand so Cam can study the in-situ version," said Squid.

I kicked myself; I should've thought of that. After Squid collected a sample, we each dug up a handful or two of stones. The colors and internal markings ranged widely, and spoke to me. My mind filled with painting ideas.

"We need to continue our journey," said Squid, interrupting my reverie.

"Of course. We should be back at our starting point fairly soon," I said.

We started walking and a moment later my foot slipped. Glancing down, an area not covered with the usual brownish vegetation appeared. I knelt and brushed at the surface.

"I've found something. Any guesses?" I had a good idea what my discovery implied, but I didn't want to give them any suggestions.

"We need to uncover more of the surface before I can offer any opinion," said Squid.

"Yes," Tyne agreed.

For once, the boys agreed, so we chopped away at the ground covering. With the visible open spots and the area uncovered after our attack, we all came to the same conclusion—we'd found a pathway about eight feet wide.

"We need to get back," I said. "This news needs to be passed along."

Tyne gazed off into the distance.

"*life circle,*
emerging,
path to understanding."

I didn't have a clue about Tyne's explanation, but now was not the time for a quiz. "Squid?"

"Oh, no question. Onwards and upwards."

"Very funny, Squid. There's no way I'm climbing any more mounds today," I said.

"Not what I meant. I…"

I interrupted. "Let's continue along our chosen circle at double speed. We should be fairly close to our starting point."

Squid gave me the evil eye, but I ignored him.

Back at the mounds, I ran up to Major Craig. "Lots to report, Major. We found a bunch of interesting things."

"*Things* is not an informative word, Mile, and neither is *bunch*." Sylone smiled and then turned around and shouted. "Okay, everyone, finish what you're doing and pack up. It's time to go back for dinner and a debriefing."

Then Mom turned back to me. "I look forward to your team's report, Mile. Sounds like you had a great afternoon."

The three of us helped pack up, and then we returned. We all took an hour to clean up and write our reports, and then we gathered for dinner. Afterwards, we cleared the tables, and settled down for our meeting.

"The most-eventful-day award goes to Mile and her team," said Major Craig. "Tell us about your adventures."

I glanced at Tyne and Squid, but they indicated I should provide the information. "Let me send everyone a copy of my report." I waited for a moment for the document to arrive, and then said, "To summarize, we discovered another set of mounds. Their shapes are a little wider at the base and flatter on top, but pretty consistent with the first set. These mounds are near a pond. On a secondary circular search, a little further out, we discovered what we believe is a path. We found an area lined with the equivalent of paving stones. The path needs to be explored. Who knows where it leads?"

Sylone let the conversation flow. Then she said, "Any questions?"

Cam piped up. "Did you take lots of samples?"

Squid said, "I deposited all our samples, suitably labeled, in your lab."

"Perfect. Your path grabbed my attention, though. Why do you think it's man-made? Well, alien-made, I guess."

We all laughed at his words. "After discovering a portion of the ground devoid of vegetation, we noticed how relatively smooth it was. So we scrubbed away at the surface and found other flat stone-like pieces. Looked like paving stones to all of us. And the pattern didn't seem to be random. Look at my report, I've added photos." I'd tried to be thorough.

"Excellent. Any other questions?" asked Sylone.

I asked, "Did you find anything at the mounds?" after no one responded to Major Craig. What had we missed while exploring?

"One of the other mounds held the same items as the first cache discovered by the Keeki," said Major Craig. "We've brought everything back for analysis but our initial brief study didn't reveal anything new. However, we now have our own copy of the written plates left by the owners. I'll be sending photos back to Earth so our linguists can have some fun."

Laughter bounced around the tables, and conversations began. Interrupting, Major Craig said, "In honor of the discoveries of Mile's team, I've decided there'll be no exploring tomorrow."

Questions erupted, so Sylone held up a hand, and we quieted. "We all need a day of rest, so I'm declaring tomorrow a holiday. Relax and get refreshed. The next few days will be long and exhausting."

Tyne, Squid, and I started our goof-off time by indulging in games.

Squid and I presented our solutions to the previous nonogram, and Tyne agreed with our conclusions.

"What is this supposed to be?" I asked Tyne. "Is it just a random design, or is it meant to represent an item, of some sort?"

"Simple."

Which could mean anything. I decided to leave it alone, and asked, "Do you have another nonogram?" I asked Tyne. "Something a little harder, perhaps?"

He whipped out some paper and presented a copy to each of us. And then he went around the break room and offered the puzzle to everyone else.

"Tyne, this is a much more difficult puzzle. And I thank you for that; I need to stretch my brain. Can you give us a clue if any picture is involved, or just some random design?" I really wanted a clue, especially since this nonogram appeared much harder.

"*heart flower,*
simmering,
design of fame," he responded.

His kaiku gave me no usable ideas, so I decided to focus on the word *flower*.

Squid and I worked on the nonogram for a while—a fascinating puzzle, actually, and then when our brains had fizzled, we ended our day with a game of *Ticket to Ride*.

****

The next morning, after breakfast, I found a corner of the break room and set up my easel and started painting. Having a day off, and spending it in my room had no appeal.

"Question?" asked Tyne, pointing at my canvas. Surfacing, I glanced at my watch; a couple of hours had passed.

"I'm creating an image of the pond we found yesterday. I'm including the background and some of the pebbles we picked up. It won't be a totally realistic picture; I just want to give the impression of what we encountered—a way of remembering what we saw."

Tyne studied my picture but didn't utter a word.

"It's not finished yet," I said, embarrassed. I should've painted in my room if I'd wanted privacy.

To change his focus, I asked, "What kind of artistic endeavors do Keeki have?"

"Many," Tyne answered.

"Tell me about one," I said. Tyne really needed to learn how to reveal information.

"*painted designs,*
covering,
Keeki skin parts."

Chapter Four

closeness, friendship
relishing
solving puzzles together

My interpretation of Tyne's words astounded me. "You paint like this," I said, waving my hand at my canvas, "on Keeki skin?"

Tyne moved his head, and then focused on my face.

I assumed his movement indicated yes. "Why?" I asked. A form of communication?

"*colorful images,*
expressing,
emotions and feelings," Tyne said.

He reached out and took hold of my hand with one of his. Three fingers and an opposing thumb touched my skin.

Smoother than expected, this time I detected a hint of lemon in addition to the scents previously experienced. I hadn't touched Keeki skin before, and the experience unnerved me.

Then I realized I probably had—when Tyne carried me back to base after being rendered unconscious. Nothing I remembered, though.

"Permission?"

Talking myself into a corner, I asked, "You want to paint on my hand?"

"*intention positive,*
affirmation,
to create image."

An expectant look appeared—at least, that's how I interpreted his expression. Not wanting to inflict any damage on species relations, I nodded.

"Retrieve," Tyne said, and left the room.

In a moment, he returned with his own box of supplies. The container, covered in drawings, attracted my attention. "Tyne, did you paint those designs?" I pointed to his box.

He smiled; pleased with my attention, I assumed.

"*design application,*
relaxing,
quiet time hobby."

"And a fine hobby, it is. Painting helps me relax too and, I think, opens my mind to possibilities." To satisfy my curiosity, I peeked in his box. "Are these paints permanent or washable?"

"Question?" Tyne turned towards Mist, his fellow Keeki, but she didn't speak. Mist had few words, at the best of times.

"I mean, will I be able to remove your art later?" After uttering those words, I gave myself a mental smack. Had I just insulted Tyne?

"*not liking,*
designs,
easy to remove."

Tyne didn't meet my eyes.

Had I upset him? Then I glanced at Mist. Her easily recognizable laughter annoyed me. "Well, I do need to shower occasionally. Anyway, let's get on with it."

Again my comments came across as annoyed, and I recognized my failings. I definitely needed to work on my delivery.

Tyne organized his supplies and asked me to hold onto a soft ball so the skin on the back of my hand stretched. I stared off into space as he painted.

In a short time, intricate designs similar to cursive writing covered my hand. A plethora of orange and brown hues wandered in patterns, and some of the colors were hard to describe, at least by my human vision. I studied my hand and tried to decipher his painting technique—I should have watched as he painted.

"Finished," said Tyne. He went to the sink to clean his brushes.

After realizing the rest of the crew in the break room watched Tyne and me, I got up to clean my own brushes. Enough painting for today.

After my brushes were done, I turned to Tyne, who'd remained in the kitchen area.

I clenched my hand and studied his design. "Tyne, this is beautiful! I had no idea you were such an accomplished artist."

My hand painting was full of wondrous colors and intricate designs. The orange and brown tones contained hints of red and green, and the designs reminded me of fractals. Mathematical designs I held dear to my heart.

"So what images were you trying to depict?" I asked, glancing again at my hand.

Tyne didn't answer immediately. I decided to outwait his indecision.

Eventually he said,

"*friendship and comrades,*
evoking,
learning, accepting, closeness."

With an inkling of his emotions, I decided to ignore them for now.

"I think I'm going to pack a lunch and go for a walk; I'm desperately in need of exercise. Anyone want to join me?" I asked, not looking at Tyne.

"Not this time, Mile. Even though I could use exercise, I think I'm going to nap the afternoon away. I feel like I'm behind on my rest," said Cam. "I'm sure Major Craig will keep us busy the next few days." Cam grinned at Sylone.

My mother did indeed keep us busy most of the time. Her finger on the group's pulse indicated when we needed a diversion. *Does she understand Keeki needs?*

Similar sentiments echoed throughout the break room, except for Squid, Mist, and Tyne. My fellow cadets decided to join me, so the four of us packed day bags and reconvened outside our landed ship. "Where shall we walk?" I asked. "Any ideas?"

Tyne pointed in the direction opposite to our first discovered mounds.

No one objected, so we took off and walked on ground cover similar to yesterday's. I took a closer look—the grass appeared just as lifeless. Our journey took us to a wide grove of trees where we debated entering the gloom.

"Does anyone think we should go around?" I asked. "Will we get lost if we go through those trees?"

Tyne studied the grouping, and then said, “Pathfinder,” pointing to his com.

True, our coms could keep track of our journey if we set up the application.

“*colors, shapes,*
exploring,
trees, plants, life.”

I thought Tyne’s words suggested we explore the grove, but Squid disagreed. After much discussion, we reached a compromise. Tyne and I started off towards the left side of the grove, and Mist and Squid started exploring the right. As long as we kept track of our wanderings, I didn’t really care if it was west, or east, or north, or south.

Enough light descended through the grove’s canopy to enable us to walk confidently. The light from the Needles sun gave the trees a golden glow, and the ground covering almost appeared luminescent. We walked slowly and studied the vegetation. Although the previous areas encountered had few types of plant life, this location teemed.

“The flowers are quite small,” I commented. “What’s the vegetation like on your planet?” I asked Tyne.

“Varied,” he said, stopping to retrieve a drink from his pack.

I gave myself a virtual smack to the head. “Of course. Do your plants have flowers? What do they look like? Are any of them similar to these?” I bent down to pick a flower, but I found my hand grabbed.

“What’re you doing?” I asked. Was Tyne attacking me?

“*no gloves,*
possible,
poisonous to touch,” said Tyne, pulling me to my feet.

Probably an over-reaction, but our previous sampling had been with gloved hands, in case the vegetation would affect us, and I should’ve known better. My unconscious episode remained to haunt me.

I sighed. “Thank you, Tyne. You’ve saved me again.” My emotions slid between extremes—his nearness and my stupidity. I messaged Mist and Squid to remind them to use gloves when sampling—even though we weren’t a real away team today, and I wasn’t in charge. Just a little bossy to cover my embarrassment.

Tyne and I continued walking and studying the foliage. Lots of strange shaped plants greeted us. As we progressed, the colors of the vegetation began to increase in boldness, and the plants appeared more invigorated. A brightness appeared in the distance, and I realized we must be closing in on the edge of the grove. As we continued our stroll the vegetation began to lose its luster. Although the Keeki had fewer words than humans, his silence surprised me.

Breaking out into the sunshine, I spied a vast field rolling towards the horizon. The two of us walked further and came upon what I could only conclude was a pile of *stuff.*

Ignoring the mound before me, I said, "Tyne, look over there," pointing with my right hand. "There's something shining in the sun." Very indistinct, at this distance, but shiny, nonetheless.

"Yes," he said, after glancing where my hand pointed. Then he turned back and studied me.

"*gather together,*
exploring,
away team join."

Pondering his kaiku, I eventually understood he wanted Mist and Squid to join us and become a team. So I called them.

Tyne and I waited until Mist and Squid exited the forest. I explained what I thought our plan of attack should be.

After a lack of objections, I asked, "What do you make of that pile?"

Mist and Squid walked around the mound taking a closer look.

"I think we have a garbage heap," said Squid. "There are broken bits of metal and plastic. I'm guessing here, but Cam should be able to confirm. And the whole pile is kind of smelly."

"Did the unknown owners of Needles leave these deposits? Or perhaps another group?" I mused. "No matter, Major Craig will be delighted with our finds. Let's take close up pictures before we continue."

We puttered about the heap for a while, and then started off in the direction of the shininess. We soon stumbled across an area of frizzled ground cover.

"This is like that patch we found on yesterday's excursion," said Squid.

"*similar pattern,*
exposing,

vegetation in pain," said Tyne.

"Like your unhappy tree?" I asked. None of us could forget Tyne's statement. A great number of Keeki pronouncements confused me, but that one concerned me. I really wanted to understand what Tyne meant.

Tyne pointed back towards the grove we'd left, and said, "Unhappy."

I looked back and realized his truth. The trees on the outer edge had the similar sad look previously encountered.

"Well, let's see what that shiny area's all about. Some of our questions may be answered," I commented.

We walked for a bit then came across the shiny ground. The area reminded me of a large pad with a black, reflective, covering. One by one, the four of us cautiously stepped on the flat surface.

"What could this be?" asked Squid. "It seems too perfect; there's not even a leaf or piece of dirt on the surface."

I backed off onto normal ground. "Not only that, my feet were starting to warm."

The other three glanced down and also retreated a few steps.

"What's that all about?" I asked. "Where's that warmth coming from? Were we being fried by microwaves? What's keeping the surface clean?"

"You know what I think?" asked Squid, "This is a landing pad, so the surface needs to be kept clear."

We ruminated on his words. "You may be right, but let's leave the analysis for the rest of the team. We should probably get back with our findings." I sighed. "If nothing else, I'd like a nap before dinner."

Mom's deduction about a required rest day had been spot on.

The four of us increased our pace and returned to the ship in record time. We dumped our samples in the lab, and retired to our rooms. I sent Major Craig a message recounting our findings before I fell asleep.

In too short a time, I heard a knock at my door. "Dinner?" asked Squid.

I looked at my watch and scowled at the passage of time. "I need a shower. I'll meet you in the break room."

The last to arrive, I rummaged up dinner and sat beside Tyne. Changing his working uniform, he now wore a garish outfit similar to coveralls. Interesting to me, the designs on his garment reflected the back of my hand. I needed to find out about the underlying structure and meanings of Keeki art.

"Mile, now that your unofficial away team is all accounted for, how about enlightening us on what your group discovered today," said Major Craig.

"Diagram," interrupted Tyne. He pecked at his com.

A bunch of pings indicated receipt of a document. Tyne had sent a drawing of today's path and objects. His artistic talents showed.

"Thanks, Tyne. This'll make my report easier to understand." So I discussed the mound of debris, the crop circles, and the flat, shiny pad we'd found.

"Your recreational exercise paid off," said Sylone. "We might have to keep sending you guys out exploring."

Cam jumped in. "What do you think that mound of stuff is all about?"

"The consensus seems to be a garbage heap. We saw broken items of all shapes and sizes and what was most likely compost from discarded food," I said. "A bit smelly, actually."

A revelation! If the compost heap smelled, then the aliens' visit had been recent.

My burning questions consisted of who, and where were they now?

Our unofficial away team was quizzed on all manner of details while I tried to eat.

Finally, Cam said, "Well I, for one, want to go dig in that garbage pile tomorrow. Who knows what I'll find." He sighed.

"Nothing, actually," answered Sylone.

Cam frowned at her. Major Craig laughed and said, "Tomorrow, we're going to trundle out to the pond and investigate all the things Mile and her team found. The garbage heap can wait."

A crestfallen look appeared on Cam's face, so I said, "You have our samples from today to work on. They should be able to give you an idea of what we discovered."

He sat up straighter and zoned out. My ploy worked. Mom gave me a sly glance. She recognized my antics.

Briny piped up. "Tyne, can you tell us anything about what you drew on Mile's hand? The design is interesting."

He didn't answer, so Briny asked, "Mist, can you enlighten us?"

Mist shook her head as if saying no, but a strange expression appeared on her face. For some reason, I got the impression she was uncomfortable with the topic of hand painting.

The humans glanced at the Keeki in the break room but no one spoke.

I thought about Tyne and his hand painting until, to relieve the tension, my mother asked, "Mile, would you teach Major White and me the game you were playing last night? Something about trains, I believe."

So we cleared a table and set up *Ticket to Ride*. Tyne and Cam joined Sylone and John White and me. Other games appeared and the whole crew of twenty, human and Keeki, topped off our rest day by having a pleasant game night.

While we cleaned up after our second game of *Ticket to Ride*, Tyne asked, "puzzle?"

Sylone sent a questioning glance my way.

"A few of us have been investigating a puzzle, a logic puzzle I guess you could call it. Quite interesting. Tyne's been teaching us. Let me grab some samples and paper. I'll be right back."

I ran to my room and gathered up supplies.

"Tyne, correct me when I'm wrong, please," I said, before giving instructions and a sample to Sylone and Major White. I let them try our original puzzle, and they picked it up right away.

"Now, Tyne has been such an inspiration and, it turns out, most of us love puzzles, so we've been making up our own. Tyne says the Keeki have competitions but we haven't yet looked into how they would work with this group. Anyway, I made up a couple of my own. This is a fifteen by fifteen, and will take some time. So what we usually do is work on them when we have can, and then gather together in the evenings to see what people have accomplished. Let me give you copies of my latest puzzle."

I instructed the printer in the break room to make copies and passed them around to whoever wanted one.

The break room became quiet. A pleasant quiet, though.

Before I started on another puzzle, I presented my solution of the last one given to us.

"*closeness, friendship,*
relishing,
solving puzzles together."

He touched the back of my hand covered with his drawings. His comment about closeness gave me much to think about.

I reluctantly broke eye contact and looked around the break room.

Games abounded, so I continued the fun. People got snacks and drinks and worked on their endeavors for a couple of hours.

"Mile, this puzzle is quite interesting and I'm enjoying it, but I have a few reports to write. See everyone in the morning. We have another long day," said Major Craig.

Major Craig and Major White stood and left at the same time. They walked closely together; their shoulders touched, and their gazes met.

A couple? My mother and John?

Chapter Five

green concern
unhappy
lack of power

A couple? Mom and Major White? Did my imagination create their entwined hands?

You just don't want to think the thoughts, I told myself.

Although I knew Mom had pursued relationships after she and my father broke up, for some reason romance for anyone on this trip surprised me. Probably unrealistic; romance always emerged and, usually, most unexpectedly.

I returned my attention to my puzzle, but I soon realized nonograms didn't catch my attention tonight. I needed a diversion. "Does anyone want a game of *Uno*?"

From the puzzled looks I received, particularly from Tyne and Mist, I needed to provide an explanation. "*Uno* is a fairly simple card game. You need to match the previous played card's color or number. If you can't, you draw a card. The object of the game is to be the first to get rid of all of your cards. Of course, there are special cards like Wild, Skip, Reverse." Any confusion on the faces slipped away after my explanation, so I said, "Somebody find out who wants to play while I run and get my deck."

After I returned from my cabin, Tyne, Mist, Cam, and Squid were waiting. Over the course of a couple of games, the Keeki became enthusiastic. And finding out Tyne and Squid loved to play Skip and Reverse amused me. A little male competitiveness, perhaps.

While we played, Squid asked, "Why do you like games so much, Mile? It certainly appears like you do."

"I don't really know. Probably because they keep my brain active, and they allow me glimpses into other people's souls."

"Souls?" asked Tyne, a skeptical look on his face. Humans I could read, most of the time, unlike the Keeki.

"Well, maybe *souls* isn't the right word." I didn't want to discuss the concept of religion with humans or Keeki. "Perhaps understanding people's behavior and actions might be a better description."

No one commented, but a lot of glances flew around the table.

"And I think I get inspiration from playing games," I continued.

"Inspiration?" asked Cam. "Inspiration for what? Puzzles?"

"Oh, ideas for my painting; directions to explore; stuff like that."

Again no one commented, but their faces indicated their interest.

Eventually, our evening wound down since tomorrow would involve a long day of exploration.

Again Squid waited for me to leave, so we could walk to our rooms together. His new habit irritated.

"Mile, can we explore together tomorrow?" asked Squid.

His desire to spend time with me gave me an uncomfortable feeling. However, since I had little experience regarding relationships, perhaps I'd misinterpreted his words.

So all I said was, "Let's see what Major Craig decides in the morning," and scurried into my cabin.

****

After breakfast, the exploration crew piled into the rover and we trundled out to the set of four mounds discovered yesterday by our team of cadets.

Happily, Sylone put the cadets together for another excursion. Not so happily, in my opinion, she told Squid to lead the away team. We all needed the experience, but Squid had acted a little weird lately, in my opinion.

The four of us walked a few feet away from the mounds. "Okay, guys," said Squid, "let's follow the stone path we discovered."

Before we reached the path, I stopped at the pond and started picking up additional pebbles for my collection.

"Not now, Mile," said Squid. "We'll get some on our way back. I want to get a few hours of exploring in, first."

Grumbling internally, I glanced at Tyne and Mist. Neither gave any indication they disagreed with Squid's pronouncement, so I stood and followed along at the rear of our group.

We soon encountered the stone path. Surprisingly comfortable, I turned my gaze to our surroundings. Beyond a wide streak of sand on both sides of the path, I saw short trees with minimal ground cover. The vegetation today included colors of red and orange.

"You know, guys," I said, "this plant life is looking a little stressed. What do you think?"

"*green concern,*
unhappy,
lack of power," said Tyne.

Squid and I stared at Tyne.

I had no clues regarding Tyne's words, but I wondered if Squid understood?

"The ground is getting drier and drier," commented Squid. "I wonder if there's a shortage of water around here."

Ping! "That reminds me of our excursion yesterday. You know, that scorched area we came upon that looked like crop circles." Of course, crop circles required a detailed explanation for the Keeki.

"Nothing," said Mist, glancing at Tyne.

I assumed she meant the Keeki didn't have anything like the unexplained circles or designs encountered. What information did our databases have about the Keeki home world?

However, I needed to pull myself back to the present. "I agree, Squid. The area's getting drier. Were any aerial surveys done before we landed? By a previous team, perhaps? The EEF?"

Squid just shook his head, and gestured for us to continue our trek. No information had been in our briefings.

We soon came upon an archaeological find delighting everyone. Beside our path, we found an area filled with stones of various sizes and shapes. An apparent pattern teased us, as I could almost hear the thoughts bouncing off the walls of the minds surrounding me. However, no one ventured any opinions as to meaning or purpose.

"This reminds me of a puzzle," I said. "One I'm sure we expert puzzle solvers will have no problem deciphering. Obviously, we can't pick the stone pattern up and take it with us, but we can certainly document the daylights out of it."

So that's what we did. Patterns swirled through my mind and interfered with other thoughts. I really was addicted to puzzles.

"Okay, let's travel a bit further, and then stop for an early lunch. I want to see a good deal more of this countryside on today's excursion," said Squid.

While we walked, the area surrounding our path became drier and drier. The foliage colors got darker and darker which may have indicated a lack of moisture.

Eventually, we came to a spot on the path where the trees beside us disappeared, and a large, flat-topped rock rose from the ground—a perfect spot to stop and rest.

I glanced back at the ground traversed, while I rummaged in my pack for food and drink. "Why is this path here? I haven't seen any evidence of inhabitants. And I don't think you can call that garbage heap we found yesterday, a sign of habitation. The people who buried those annoying plates probably just left their garbage behind."

"Irresponsible," said Mist.

I agreed with her sentiment, and gave her a nod. "Squid?"

"You're right. I haven't seen anything today to indicate this planet was ever inhabited—except for this path, and the mounds, of course. No homes, no nothing. This path is quite an anomaly."

I glanced at Tyne.

"*further answers,*
searching,
more exploration required."

Yup, that's what we were here for—exploration.

The four of us took a quiet, almost silent, lunch. Our trip, so far today, gave us much to think about. After taking the last bite of my sandwich, I said pointing, "Looks like a bunch of low hills. Why don't we do a little jogging to get there as soon as possible?"

We started off at a leisurely pace—after all, we were still digesting our lunches. At least the humans were—the Keeki's internal organs remained a mystery.

Only a short time passed before we reached the hills. "Looks like some kind of pyramids to me," I said. "What a strange design to find on an alien world. Maybe the previous inhabitants contacted Earth in the past."

"Unlikely," said Squid.

When did he become an expert? Was he there? I soon gave myself a lecture about my crankiness. At least, my thoughts had been internal.

"Tyne, Mist, do you have pyramid-like structures on Keeki?" I asked.

"*ancient buildings,*

indicating,

…"

"Mist and I will search these two," said Squid, interrupting Tyne. "Mile, you and Tyne investigate the further two pyramids."

Frustrated with Squid's interruption of Tyne's kaiku, I decided to wait until later to ask.

As Tyne and I took off towards the two we were to explore, Squid said, "Be quick, as we need to start back fairly soon."

The monuments appeared to be about thirty feet high, with a thirty foot square footprint, I determined, as we got closer.

Tyne and I travelled around the base of the farthest pyramid. No vegetation was evident and inches of yellow dust covered the sides of the pyramids and the ground. We found no openings or other marks, but we dutifully recorded our limited findings.

We walked over to our second pyramid. As Tyne and I approached the back side, I noticed less dust on this particular pyramid. Before we could investigate any of the other three sides, we discovered an entrance at the back. Tyne ran off to tell Squid and Mist, after making me promise to stay outside.

While I saw Tyne talking to Squid and Mist, I glanced at the entrance. Moats of dust floated in the air. I reached out with my right hand and touched some resistance. Pushing a little harder, my hand slowly breached the barrier.

Chapter Six

discovering topics
exploring
human-Keeki relationships

"Mile, take it easy. Just slowly open your eyes. You're hooked up to an IV, so don't thrash about."

Briny's familiar calm voice eased my urge to jump up. "Why am I in the infirmary?" I asked, after glancing at my surroundings.

"What do you last remember?" she asked, while taking my blood pressure and ignoring my question.

I tried to see my blood pressure reading, but she kept her body between me and the machine. *What do I remember?* "Oh, our team found some pyramids. Four, to be exact. Tyne and I were investigating two of them, and Squid and Mist the others. Tyne and I found one with an entrance, so Tyne ran off to tell Squid. I just stood at the entrance and waved my hand around. I didn't go in." Still embarrassed from my earlier incident, I wanted everything perfectly clear. "So why am I here?"

"Because you lost consciousness again. At least, you're consistent," said a grinning Briny. "You'll be fine. I've taken blood samples, but I suspect you were subjected to the same gas as before."

"But I didn't go inside!" I objected.

"No, but the general consensus is you broke some kind of force field, and the gas inside escaped and surrounded you." Briny put away the blood pressure machine.

"Well, I do remember feeling some sort of membrane, or resistance, at the entrance to the pyramid. How did I get back to the ship?"

"Oh, the usual. Squid called Major Craig, and Tyne carried you to meet the rover. And then he came along in the rover and slung you over his shoulder and brought you in here." I was sure Briny identified the horrified look on my face, because she said, "Just kidding. You looked quite sweet in his arms, though." She laughed. "And then the rover went back to pick up the others."

"I'm in so much trouble, Briny. What am I going to do? Why's this happening to me, and no one else?"

Briny declined to answer, as my mother had stepped into the infirmary.

"Mile, you can sit up but be still for a little while. Then you should be good to go. This gas doesn't seem to have any side effects. And now I need to get to Supplies and pick up a few things." A small smile graced her face, as she left.

My mother came over and helped me up, and then gave me a hug. "I'm sorry, Mom. I really didn't go through the pyramid's entrance; I just waved my hand around."

"I know. Tyne told me he found you slumped on the ground outside. You do get in some predicaments, don't you?" commented Sylone.

I heard the fondness in her voice; the love she couldn't express around the others.

"However, I do have to include the incident in my report to headquarters. Don't worry; you won't get a reprimand on your record."

"I'm really not trying to make your life difficult," I said. Things just seemed to happen to me.

"You have an inquisitive nature, Mileena," she replied. "One of your endearing qualities, actually. Now, go write your report—if you feel up to it. We'll have lots to discuss at dinner tonight." My mother gave me a peck on the cheek and another hug, and left the infirmary.

I spent thirty minutes in my cabin writing my report—a surprisingly easy exercise today. Experience did make tasks go quicker.

At dinner, Major Craig outlined the findings from the second set of mounds. In one mound, another similar four-sectioned artifact was uncovered containing our second set of tablets, with exactly the same inscriptions as the first. The other three sections had no surprises. Pretty much a duplicate set of mounds. The team did excavate the remaining three mounds but nothing new was uncovered. All in all, an unremarkable excavation.

"Did the people who left the tablets also create the mounds?" I asked.

"Unlikely. The mounds appear to have been here quite a while. And each mound, where tablets were found, had obviously been disturbed," said Cam, "so they were easy to discover. Particularly the one you fell into." Cam laughed and laughed, and tears ran down his face.

With a reproving glance, Sylone continued. "Many samples were taken from the pond and the surrounding area; enough to keep Cam busy for a long, long time."

He wouldn't look at anyone, so I decided her message had landed.

"Squid, tell us what your team found today," continued Major Craig.

He picked up his com. "Let me send everyone a copy of my report." After a moment, he continued, "We started on the path we'd discovered the previous day, and it continued for some distance. In fact, we never got to the end. As we walked along, we discovered an area on the ground, beside the path, scattered with stones. There were individual ones, and various piles. Some kind of puzzle, or maybe an indicator of some sort. You'll see the pictures in my report." Squid glanced at his notes. "And we noticed our surroundings getting drier and drier as we continued."

"So what was the vegetation like?" asked Briny.

I answered. "The foliage, to begin with, had hues of red and orange, then the colors began to get darker and darker. The trees became shorter and, eventually, we came upon a desert. And then the pyramids appeared."

"I know you've taken lots of pictures but describe the pyramids from your perspective, Mile," said Major Craig.

"I'd say about thirty feet tall, and thirty feet square, at the base. Kind of a dirty brown color and covered in a thick layer of dust. The surfaces, sides, whatever you want to call them, were covered with slight ridges or knobs. We only found one area that appeared to be an entrance—I mean Tyne and I found one. Squid, did you and Mist find any openings?"

He shook his head. A little disappointed, I gathered.

"And no one saw anything inside the pyramid?" asked Sylone.

"No, too dark," said Squid. "And we wanted to get Mile back to Briny, before the skies fell, or something." He waved his hand around.

A little laughter ensued, and embarrassment flashed over me again.

Sylone took a sip of coffee. "Tomorrow, we're going to stick together since we have a lot of area to cover. In the morning, we're going to check out what the cadets discovered on our day off—the garbage pile, and such. Then in the afternoon, it's off to the pyramids. While we're investigating them, the ship is going to relocate to Base 2. So, when we've finished our tasks, we'll bundle into the rover and meet *Skyfall*—rather than returning to Base 1. Any questions?"

No one commented, so Major Craig said, "Enjoy your evening, and let's get an early start." We received orders regarding our leaving time, and what to pack for the day.

Tyne, Squid, Mist, and I'd all sat at the same table tonight. So, as we finished up our food, Squid said, "I want to have a discussion regarding away team protocol. For example, Mile, you shouldn't have entered the pyramid on your own."

"I didn't enter; I didn't broach the door; I did *nothing*. All I did was wave my arm around. How was I to know a membrane, or something, held back my favorite obnoxious gas." I glared at Squid; actually, I glared at everyone. "And, besides, you would have all been gassed if we'd been together, so I don't think you're being very logical."

"Okay, okay," said Squid, holding up his hands in surrender. "I just wanted to remind everyone about protocol, in case we're on the same away team again."

Protocol? Squid was a little confused, but I decided not to vocalize my words.

However, I did think some of them—such a smart ass, and coming across as a little too self-important. Like he was the only one to ever lead an away team. I sighed, and admonished myself. We all needed to learn how to lead; my turn would come again.

"*discovering topics,*
exploring,
human-Keeki relationships," said Tyne, interrupting my self-imposed scolding.

What did he mean by his kaiku? I glanced at Mist. She hadn't said a word so far this evening. Even though the Keeki could be unreadable, this time her face expressed which human-Keeki relationship Tyne wanted to explore, and her unhappiness.

Frustration flooded my mind. I didn't bang my fist on the table, but I certainly wanted to. "Would everyone just leave me alone? I've had a bad day; I just want to relax."

To confuse me further, Mist leaned over, and put her arm around my shoulders. "Hormones," she whispered. Her reddish skin under the light blue scales had darkened.

I thought about what she'd said, and decided she probably knew Tyne, maybe Squid, and maybe even me, better than I did.

Taking a big gulp of air, I said, "Sorry, guys. I'm really, really, sorry for my outburst. I've had a stressful day, and I'm really getting tired of being gassed by noxious alien fumes." Sweat covered my body.

No one responded with any anger, so I decided they forgave my outburst.

I took a deep breath. "So what do you want to do? Work on nonograms?" My brain refused to think about any important topic.

The group agreed. Nonograms still interested everyone.

While we ate dessert and mumbled over our puzzles, Cam joined our table. "I'm going to work on that pattern of stones you found. It's fascinating. I don't know where to start and that excites me." He grinned.

"Maybe it's not a puzzle," I said. "Maybe they're just randomly deposited stones."

Cam laughed. "I don't think so; I already have ideas. I'll let you know how it goes." He walked away exhibiting a lively jaunt. Puzzles did excite his scientific brain.

I turned back to the table. "I need another nonogram to work on. Would someone please create one? Maybe something to do with our exploration?"

"Idea," said Mist.

"Great. Send me the puzzle when you get it finished," I said. As I glanced around the break room, my mother walked towards us.

"Mile, I must admit I love these puzzles. I have the solution to your latest," said Sylone.

I looked at her piece of paper and I agreed. "You do! You're the first!"

A quick thought popped into my mind. "I need to have a prize for the first person to solve one of my puzzles. I'm going to have to think about what'd be appropriate. Major Craig, your prize will be delivered a little later." Laughter filled the air. "I'll get cracking on making new puzzles, too. Perhaps derived from this planet."

My mind turned to puzzles while Mom waved a goodbye. She and Major White left the break room together.

Okay, my previous impression remained but, today, the revelation didn't bother me. Apparently, I'd only needed a small adjustment in my way of thinking about my mother.

Most of our expedition crew still remained in the break room. Conspicuous by his absence was Aran Silo, the Keeki leader. I didn't remember him recently participating in any games or puzzles. Would he not want to keep an eye on the Keeki?

The evening wore on. We played games and solved puzzles. A pleasant time, but my energy eventually dissipated.

"I need to get some rest," I said. "Maybe because of my gassing, but I'm pretty pooped."

Mist and Squid left together, and only Tyne and I remained.

"Walk?" asked Tyne.

"Yes, it's time to retire. I'm tired." His motive eluded me, but walking together remained my best guess.

At my cabin door, Tyne touched my forehead. "Like?" he asked.

His soft, slightly oily fingers soothed, so I said, "Yes. Very nice."

Tyne rubbed my forehead a bit, and then commented, "Smell like Major Craig."

Could he really recognize our relationship? Or maybe that's not what he meant? Maybe he thought all human females smelled the same?

"Stones." Startling me, he grabbed one of my hands and dumped a mound of stones in my palm.

"Thank you. I'd love to add these to my collection." Words failed me—he'd caught me off guard.

"*enjoy sleep,*

tomorrow,

discoveries to unfold." A small smile graced his face. Keeki smiles weren't hard to recognize—the corners of their mouths sparkled.

I smiled back, but turned to my room to end our encounter. Tyne really did want to explore human-Keeki relations.

Chapter Seven

information tablets
revealing
only source available

The next morning, Major Craig decreed we all needed more exercise, so we'd walk to the garbage site, instead of taking the rover. No one complained—at least, not out loud.

During our journey through the grove, I took a closer look at the foliage. The colors changed from a blue-green hue to a yellow-orange, as we progressed along the path. And on today's excursion, the encroaching dryness was strongly evident.

Reaching the garbage dump, the excitement level rose. Apparently, everyone loved rummaging and looking for treasure. We hoped we'd find the answer to one of our burning questions—the identity of the aliens who planted the stone tablets.

For our sample taking, Cam and Briny handed out various sized sealable plastic bags. Suitably gloved, I went dumpster diving. I found a lot of biodegradable items, and numerous smells—mostly unrecognizable. Obviously, these particular visitors had arrived recently. I dutifully took samples, and then went on to the more interesting, and hopefully more informative, items. I found container shaped items, and what I thought were eating utensils. An item, perhaps a knife, had a handle riddled with holes. A great deal of plastic-like items permeated the area where I dug. And then I found my motherlode—a huge pile of pebbles. I gathered up as many as possible. Cam would be given the word any excess belonged to me. I wondered how he'd take that pronouncement.

Cam had brought along four inflatable wheeled containers, so we assembled his contraptions and filled them with our samples, as the morning progressed.

Eventually, Major Craig said, "Okay, it's time to proceed to the area Mile described as a crop circle. We may return and investigate this pile, at a later time, if the samples we've gathered warrant it," added Major Craig, after Cam jerked up and opened his mouth to protest.

After this morning, no one argued with our away team's description of a garbage dump. Now, how would they react to my crop circle image?

The group walked around the pattern. Cam and Briny took samples, and stored them away.

"This isn't exactly a circle," said Major Craig. "More oblong, like the bottom of a boat."

She'd seen the image clearer than I had.

"Like the bottom of a spaceship," commented Major White.

We all glanced his way. That image had eluded us. "Is that why it's beside this other area? We think it's a heated landing pad."

"You may be correct. Ships landing, and then moving away so others can land, is a viable explanation," said Sylone.

Cam took samples and agreed with us the temperature of the smooth surface indicated heating by an unknown source. "The texture is not exactly concrete, but is certainly a substance repelling other matter."

"Why would it be heated?" I asked. "How does it work?" My mind filled with questions.

"Second question, probably solar heating," said Cam. "First question: heated to keep the surface clear of debris for landings. I can think of better ways, but I may be totally off base."

We all glanced at the pad, but no one had any other revelations.

"Okay, time to return to base and grab a quick lunch. Then we'll take the rover to the pyramids," said Major Craig.

The run back to our ship didn't take long because we were wound up, and lunch took little time. In the rover, everyone sported a smile. Apparently, pyramids contained one of the keys to happiness.

While we traveled to the pyramids' location, Major Craig assigned duties, and mentioned the high intensity lamps brought along to illuminate the insides of the ruins. They would bring the inside of the pyramid Tyne and I'd encountered to life. I did notice Mist and Squid weren't particularly happy to be ordered to take a gander around the area, rather than explore the pyramids.

Upon our arrival at the pyramids, we unloaded our equipment. Mist and Squid took off on their ramble, and the rest of us waited while Cam poked a probe inside to determine if any lingering gases remained. After he declared the air safe, we picked up the bright lamps and other tools and trotted inside.

I promptly started sneezing, and I wasn't the only one. A thick layer of dust covered everything. I stepped closer to my assigned wall, and rubbed my hand over it. After studying the surface for a few moments, I said, "I'm convinced this wall has markings. Perhaps designs or writing, but the dust is obscuring a lot. What about the other walls? What do you think they show? Can we remove the dust?" I asked Major Craig.

Mom spoke with the rest of the crew and came to the conclusion all walls carried markings. Thankfully, the floor had none so we could walk around without destroying evidence. Major Craig told everyone to don their face masks, and to gently remove the dust from the surfaces with the duster-like tools we carried for digging out archaeological finds. After the task was complete, we went outside for a break. I certainly needed food and fluid, particularly fluids.

"So what did everyone see? What do you think is on the walls?" I asked. "I need wild theories, and maybe some facts."

Laughter abounded. "I think we just found an alien porn novel," said Cam.

Silence greeted his announcement. "Really?" I asked. What a seriously weird theory.

"No, silly. What we have here is a record of some sort. I have no clue what it's all about, and I have no idea how to translate the markings. However, some of the scratches reminded me of the tablets we found," said Cam. "A scientific puzzle to solve, to be sure. And our experts—you know who you are—will be the first to find the answer, I predict."

A unique challenge, for sure. A lot of thoughtful faces from our nonogram addicts abounded.

With little data, no one disagreed with Cam's analysis. After our break, we went inside the pyramid and took more pictures, just in case.

Emerging from the gloom, I talked to Mist and Squid, who'd just returned. Evidently, Major Craig had given them permission to expand their search beyond the pyramids. I'd wondered about their absence.

"Major, we only found desert on the other side of the pyramids. So we came back and continued on the stone path, to see where it led. Didn't find anything new, so we walked back," said Squid.

"Good." Sylone thought for a moment. "So since we haven't found any more openings in the pyramids, I think our job here is done—at least for the moment. I'm going to call the ship and have them move to Base Two. We'll walk and meet them there. This path leads in the right direction."

One of the crew drove the rover, but the rest of us elected to walk. As we strode along, we all studied our desert-like surroundings. However, the wall drawings filled my thoughts, although I tried to focus on our path. After a time, vegetation began to return. Although miniature to begin with, the ground cover rapidly developed. Then trees began to appear with oak leaf shaped leaves and darker colors.

We soon came upon the clearing where our ship had landed.

"I'm sure we all need a bit of down time, so we'll discuss our findings at dinner," Major Craig announced.

We helped Cam dump our samples in his lab, and then wandered our various ways.

I took advantage of our off time for both a shower and a nap.

The break room had energy this evening. Everyone wanted to discuss the pyramids, but Major Craig made us wait. She insisted on a linear discussion. So we started with our first stop.

"I've only had time to do an initial analysis of the samples we took at the debris pile but, in my opinion, it certainly resembles a garbage dump. I'm hoping to be able to study the organic matter to determine what kind of life forms we're dealing with. And, eventually, I hope to get an understanding of the sentient lifeforms who deposited those items. But it'll all take time," said Cam.

"Are you assuming this garbage dump relates to the people who deposited the plates?" I asked.

"You're absolutely right, Mile. We shouldn't jump to conclusions," said Cam. He got a far-off look in his eyes.

"They probably are the same, though," I said. "What are the chances of more than one race?" And I had no idea on how to calculate the odds. Of course, predicting the occurrence of alien species had never been a precise science.

"Now, are there any other comments about what we found at the *hypothetical* garbage dump? Anything interesting to report, any speculations, or should we leave Cam and Briny with a few years' worth of testing?" asked Major Craig.

I glanced at the two of them. They did indeed look overwhelmed.

"One of the items I retrieved, intrigued me," I said. "Photo on the way."

While everyone studied my picture, I thought about how to approach the topic. "My first thought regarding this item was a knife riddled with holes. What do you think? Any other ideas?" I asked.

"I think you're right," said Cam. "The long part certainly looks like a knife blade. Chopping comes to mind."

"I do have an idea about why the handle has holes," I said. "Assuming, it really is a knife."

Everyone studied the six non-linear holes.

"What's your theory, Mile?" asked our scientist, Cam.

"Looking at the pattern, I think we have a thumb hole and five finger holes. One of our aliens—and I don't mean the Keeki—is six fingered."

"I'll keep your hypothesis in mind," said Cam.

"Interesting conclusion, Mile, and I'm inclined to agree," said Major Craig. "Perhaps we'll get a confirmation from another sample we've acquired."

"Anything else to bring up?" my mother asked the group. With no response, Sylone continued, "Yes, we have much to analyze." She glanced at her notes. "Now what about the crop circles, as Mile so interestingly named them?"

"They're not really circles. More oblong, as Major White pointed out." Cam said. "I did have a chance to analyze the soil and it's remarkably free of organisms. Like every living thing had been killed off."

"Why would that be?" asked Major Craig.

"I don't know, but my best guess is that a spaceship moved there after landing at the pad. And that second encounter scorched the ground in the pattern of the bottom of the ship," said Cam.

Major White agreed with his conclusion, as we all considered the implications.

"That would certainly mark the surface if they didn't wait to cool off," I said, "but why have all living organisms disappeared?"

Cam shook his head, and offered no conclusion.

"Perhaps future studies will reveal the answer," said Major Craig. She paused. "Now, I wanted you all to know I received a message from Earth, while we were out exploring."

Her comment got everyone's attention. The break room became eerily quiet.

She continued, "They've received our documents and photos. ESF will send the tablets for decoding. And they'll be definitely communicating with the Keeki ambassadors, and other representatives, to confirm our findings and the Keeki's analysis."

I glanced at our Keeki counterparts.

"Earth Sciences Force will get back to us, as soon as possible," she said.

We all laughed; *ASAP* meant different things to different groups.

"Has Earth heard about this race, these tablets?" Squid asked.

"No, they're as ignorant as we are—although they hope the Keeki representatives will have further information."

Most of the humans looked at the Keeki.

After a moment's pause, Aran said,

"*information tablets,*

revealing,

only source available."

I gathered he tried to tell us the Keeki only knew about the tablets they'd deciphered, and nothing else about our situation.

"So what are we supposed to do?" asked Cam. "Are we going home?"

"No. Well, at least not for a couple of weeks. We're to stick around here and continue to explore. The situation will be reevaluated as information is gathered."

"So, they want us to wait for whoever left the tablets?" I asked.

Major Craig didn't answer my question, but merely said, "If anyone wants to try and decipher the pyramid walls, tonight would be a good time to start. Tomorrow, we'll take a look around this new area surrounding base two."

After we cleaned up the tables, most of us stayed in the break room to work on the pyramid puzzles.

Cam went over to Major White, and then the two of them left—for places unknown. I didn't make much of it, and went back to my puzzle. Where to begin?

The break room was pretty quiet this evening, with everyone working on some puzzle or other. After an hour or so, I saw Cam and Major White return.

Then I had a revelation, “I’ve got it!” I yelled.

Chapter Eight

elevation daunting
confusion
leading to death

"But I've got it!" said Cam, throwing a frown my way.

"Something to do with the pyramid?" I asked. He'd given us no clue as to his topic, but then neither had I about mine.

"No, the pattern of stones you found," said Cam.

We stared at each other, and then both started to speak at the same time.

Major Craig interrupted. "Cam, you go first."

My mother's action annoyed me, but I couldn't decide why. Just my competitive nature, I supposed. Although I remembered she'd annoyed me yesterday, too.

Cam said, "The stone patch beside your path interested me. When I studied your photo I thought I saw a pattern. My mind went in circles for a time, and then the idea of a map popped into my head. So I asked Major White to show me visuals of Needles. We started with areas around our current location."

After the murmuring died down, Major White said, "There's a distinct possibility the stones can be interpreted as pointing to two sites."

"Where? Here on Needles?" asked my mother.

"Yes. One location is at the foot of the nearby mountains, and the other seems to indicate an ocean shore close by," said a smiling Cam. "Someone is giving us hints. Perhaps these indicators are direction signs from the previous inhabitants, or maybe from whoever left the tablets in those mounds. Maybe the stone patch and the tablets are from the same group of people. I don't know. Maybe they mean nothing but, Major, we need to check out the areas, just in case."

An anxious Cam surprised me. Usually more calm and collected when it came to scientific questions, for some reason the stone patch had resonated with him.

"Send me your information, maps, and conclusions, Cam, and I'll make a decision tonight," said Major Craig.

"Now, Mile, what do you have for us?" my mother asked.

Finally, my turn. Although Cam's information fascinated me, my anxiety had grown.

"I think one wall of the pyramid we investigated today is a dictionary to help us decipher the other walls." Creating a hardcopy picture of each wall, which included a wide border, let me scribble and attempt to understand the hieroglyphics. I took a picture of my notes and forwarded them.

"Wild leap," said Squid, after everyone spent time studying my post.

How could he come to that conclusion so quickly? Didn't he need time to analyze my scribbles and conclusions?

I decided to be tactful. "Perhaps, but study my notes. See if you agree with my interpretation of some of the characters. The wall is a pictograph like that probe we sent off into space many years ago. I'm convinced of it." Why did everyone annoy me today?

"Voyager?" asked Major White.

"Exactly." I'd read about the ancient probe somewhere—probably at the Academy.

"Mile's conjecture seems like a good project for this evening. All the puzzlers in our group should have a good time." Sylone laughed. "You may be on the right path, Mileena, or perhaps not. However, from what I've determined the last few days, everyone's on board with solving puzzles—the weirder, the better."

I heard no disagreement, and our excursion benefited from the unusual puzzles thrown our way. The problem solving had brought us closer.

Mom continued, "Tomorrow, we'll visit the mountains."

A little discussion about the mountains ensued, then the majority puzzled the rest of the evening away.

****

Of course, a bunch of us stayed up far too late solving the pyramid puzzle. The gallons of caffeine being consumed the next morning made that pretty obvious.

Today's destination, the mountain location, was nearby, so we took the rover.

The vegetation continued to be what we considered *green* for this planet. Sporadic trees outlined one side of our path and led towards the low mountain.

To my right, I decided to call the blue-green ground covering, stretching as far as I could see, a meadow. I suspected the open area led to the ocean, but only time would confirm.

As we approached the foot of the small mountain, my curiosity made me anxious to get out and explore.

However, I focused on studying our destination and the bits of sparkle I thought I saw on the side of the mountain while we drove the final stretch.

The mountain really was an oversized hill—at least, to someone who'd grown up surrounded by ski mountains and ocean. Vancouver had everything, and in such a magnificent way. Foothill was a better word for this rock outcropping.

The rover stopped close to Cam and Major White's mountain coordinates. Major Craig started splitting our group into two for forays up the hillside.

"Keeki not climb," said Aran, creating our first crisis of the day.

"Why not?" asked Major Craig, after Aran interrupted her organizing.

"*evil presence,*

residing,

gods on ground," he reiterated.

Not very informative, so I asked, "Scared of heights?"

"Cadet Carter," admonished my mother.

Surprised at her tone, I thought about my words. Meaning no criticism, I'd just wanted to understand Keeki culture. I opened my mouth to explain, but Mom motioned me silent.

"Aran, I want you to lead the Keeki on an exploration around the base of this mountain. Take food and drink and be back by late afternoon."

"Join humans?" asked Tyne.

All conversation stopped. Sylone studied her cadet. "You want to join the human away team that's going to climb the mountain?"

"*change life,*

youth,

overcoming Keeki fear," said Tyne.

Aran put his hand on the back of his neck. Usually that meant he was about to say something.

However, Mom spoke before any kaiku came our way. "You may join the human team, Tyne. If you encounter any difficulty, let someone know right away."

Aran didn't object, but simply stared at Tyne.

Trouble within the Keeki? At the very least, Tyne contradicted his leader's statements. I needed to find a way to quiz Tyne about this situation.

"Cam, in your aerial searches did you find any likely places to start our exploring?" asked Major Craig, distracting the Keeki from their staring match.

"There's a plateau I think looks promising. If we walk about fifteen minutes along the base, we'll come to a creek. From the pictures I've seen, we should have an easy walk up the creek bed. Maybe an additional forty-five minutes to reach the flat area," said Cam, pointing to his right.

I looked forward to our walk. The fresh air revealed perhaps the hint of mint, or oregano, and stimulated my senses. My mood spun upward.

Another delight involved the creek bed. As we walked along, I noticed sparks of color. At one point, I got down on my knees and scooped up a bunch of shiny pebbles—to add to my collection.

"Mile, let's keep going. You can grab a bunch on our way back," commented Major Craig.

When did my mother find out about my collection of pebbles? Actually, not a very bright question, on my part. Mothers, and expedition leaders, dug out everything.

I smiled at my thoughts, and Tyne helped me stand. Because of my mother's comment, I picked up my pace.

"Tyne, may I ask why Keeki don't like to climb?" I crossed my fingers hoping I hadn't broached a taboo subject.

"*elevation daunting,*
confusion,
leading to death."

His kaiku gave me the creeps. Did he mean Keeki died from exposure to elevation? If so, why did he wish to accompany us? And how did flying in a spaceship affect the Keeki? What about Aran's comment about *Gods on Ground*? I found the whole subject riddled with confusion. The only conclusion I could draw was I needed to keep an eye on Tyne.

"Tyne, do you like these pebbles?" I shoved my hand near his face.

He didn't comment, but he did stare at me.

What was that all about? About to quiz him, I realized we'd finally made our way up to Cam's plateau.

The greenness of the grassy area surprised me—much greener than the rest of Needles we'd encountered.

Before I could utter a comment, Major Craig said, "Let's have an early lunch."

We found various patches of grass and hunkered down. Squid and Tyne sat beside me.

"I'm curious, guys, so humor me. Squid, why did you join the ESF?" I asked.

He scowled, and didn't answer.

Not so tactful, I asked, "Squid? Don't you have anything to tell us? Surely, you love exploration or something like that?"

"Sure. Exploration is the key to the ESF," said Squid, picking at his lunch.

I decided Squid's answer had no content—especially since he stared at the grass beneath him.

So I changed my focus, "Tyne, why did you join the Keeki exploration academy? You know what I mean," I said, after he glared at me.

"*parent death,*
loneliness,
exploration releasing excitement."

This kaiku I understood and I felt bad for asking my question. *How should I respond?*

Before I spoke, Squid asked, "Both your mother and father? I'm sorry. That must have been rough."

"One," said Tyne.

After a gasp, Squid said, "You only had one parent? How does that work?"

Such a jerk. Squid robbed me of any words.

Major Craig broke up our staring match. "Let's split up. This flat area's not too large, so Tyne, Squid, Mile go around the left side, and the rest of us will wander in the opposite direction. It should only take about thirty minutes before we meet."

I really didn't want to spend any more time with Squid and Tyne—considering my chaotic thoughts—but I had no choice.

On our way around we came upon a pile of stones. "This looks like a hiding place," said Squid.

"What do you mean?" I asked.

"Just a wild guess, but I think someone's hidden information, or objects, under these stones. We need to tell Major Craig."

So we upped our pace and jogged to meet the others.

Chapter Nine

hand painting
emotions
not yet expressed

We caught up with the second group of plateau explorers. After we told Major Craig about the cairn, her eyes sparkled. My mother loved uncovering surprises.

"We need to excavate," I said. "Who knows what's under those stones?"

"Agreed. And I know all you smart people brought along the necessary equipment." Mom laughed, after we all nodded agreement. "So let's get there promptly and see what we can uncover—we still have time this afternoon."

Major Craig hesitated. "Actually, I've changed my mind."

We're not going to investigate?

"Your faces are priceless. Yes, we're going to dig out your cairn, but there are too many of us to make the excavation comfortable. Cam, please take Tyne and Squid and go back and investigate the pond we found at the top of the creek. That area looks promising."

"Tyne? Okay, so far?" asked Major Craig, while watching the trio organize themselves.

Apparently, other expedition members worried about Tyne's Keeki height response.

"Fine," Tyne responded. His skin appeared normal, and I'd heard no words of complaint during our wandering.

Tyne, Squid, and Cam took off and, after taking a million pictures around the structure, the rest of us started dismantling the cairn. Today, my assignment involved taking photographs of every stage of our deconstruction.

After we took measurements, we found the cairn to be five feet square at the base, approximately six feet tall, and its surface covered with stones.

Then came the uncovering—a fanciful word for the destruction of the structure. We'd started from the top, and about half way down we came upon a tablet.

"Now, we've found something interesting," said Major Craig. "Let's continue, but be careful. I can't see how any gasses could be trapped in the dirt, but you never know."

Again the reference; harrumph.

We continued digging out the cairn, and were rewarded with a mountain of tablets—a most delightful haul.

After a while, Cam, Tyne, and Squid returned. "We've got lots of samples," said Cam, "but we found nothing particularly notable. How about here?"

Major Craig pointed to the pile of tablets, and Cam ran over to them. "What do they say?"

"That's the million dollar question, isn't it?" she replied. "Let's pack everything up and head to the rover. Time's flown."

The Keeki away team was waiting when we reached our rendezvous.

"Let's return to base. Time for a meal," said Major Craig. "We'll debrief after dinner."

Major Craig opened the conversation. "A lot of useful and important exploration was completed today, and I thank everyone. Hopefully, tomorrow will be just as productive." She bestowed a smile on everyone in the break room. "Now, let's start with the Keeki away team. Aran, what did you discover on your tour around the mountain?"

"*creek runoff,*
residue,
landing area death," replied Aran.

"What do you mean?" I asked. "You found a landing area? Why do you think it's dead?"

"Vegetation lack," replied Aran.

His answer made some sense, I supposed. His few words did connect in a concept I understood.

"Hmm. Makes sense that whoever planted the tablets we just discovered would need to land near here, just like we did. The main question is why is this landing spot devoid of vegetation?" asked Major Craig.

A lot of silent speculation caught my attention. So many unanswered questions about Needles.

"Next up is the pond. Cam, what can you tell us?" Mom asked.

"We took lots of samples. My lab is overflowing, by the way," said Cam. He sighed. "Ignoring that situation, I have to say we found practically nothing of immediate interest. The only item of note is that the pond's shoreline is covered in Mile's pebbles. It's like this planet was designed for her—and her fainting spells." Cam laughed, but not for long after glancing at me, and then my mother.

"Now, to bring everyone up-to-date, our group found a cairn and excavated it. This artifact, the cairn, was not multi-chambered, as were the previous ones. The tablets were interspersed amongst the soil," said Major Craig.

"New characters? Any drawings?" asked Major White.

"No pictures, at least to my understanding, but much for our puzzlers to work on, I would imagine. I'll be attaching pictures of the tablets to my report to Earth this evening. Hopefully, they'll take a stab at deciphering the markings, too. In the meantime, let me send everyone copies of the tablets."

I couldn't wait to look at the pictures Mom sent. Although, I'd helped uncover the tablets, my glance had been brief. Along with the inside of the pyramid, I had an abundance of puzzles to solve today.

"Okay, I have numerous reports to write, so I'm not going to stick around this evening. However, I'd love to receive your thoughts about all the puzzles we've uncovered. We have much to teach each other."

Mom's knack of offering encouragement increased the hum in the break room. She added, "Tomorrow, we're going to investigate the ocean, and I've decided to move the ship again. Thus, we'll have an early start." She disappeared.

A few of the crew followed her action, but the majority stayed. And from the appearance of coms and paper, a lot of puzzle solving—or at least attempts—would happen. What did I want to work on? Pyramids or new tablets?

Mist sat alone at a table, so I wandered over. "Do you want to join me at that other table?" I pointed back at my working materials.

She made a movement with her body, and said, "Quiet."

"Oh, you want some quiet time. I understand. I have one question about Keeki, though. Would now be a good time to ask?"

"*Keeki interest,*
culture,
much to learn," Mist replied.

I agreed with her sentiment. Although my question might prove to be sensitive to a Keeki, I decided to ask anyway.

"You know Tyne painted on my hand." I pushed my hand towards Mist. "What does this mean? Does it signify anything? Or is it just art?"

Mist studied me for a couple of moments, then said,

"*hand painting,*
emotions,
not yet expressed."

Crystal clear. "Do you know what Tyne was saying when he painted my hand?"

"Yes."

I gave myself a mental slap. "What did Tyne attempt to express?" I asked, trying to be specific enough to receive an answer.

"Ask." She cleverly avoided answering.

What did she want to hide? I became more unsettled than ever. "I'll leave you to your quiet time. Join me, if you wish." I got up and walked back to my table, and joined Tyne and Squid.

"So, what're you guys working on?" I asked. Turned out both of them were interested in the new tablets found today.

I decided to take another look at the pyramid drawings. However, my mind refused to settle down, so I began to pack up my belongings.

"Leaving?" asked Tyne.

"Yes, I'm restless tonight. Since we're going to have an early start, I'm going to head to bed. I'll read for a while, and then I should be in the mood for sleep."

Tyne grabbed his stuff, and left before I had a chance to ask him anything. *Very strange behavior*, I thought.

So I finished packing, and started walking. Squid followed right behind; a little too close for comfort, actually, but I ignored him.

When we reached our adjoining rooms, I said, "See you tomorrow, Squid," and turned away.

Squid grabbed my arm. "Wait a moment."

"What?" I asked. My restlessness turned to annoyance.

"Will you spend the day with me tomorrow?"

Weird statement. "Well, that depends on how Major Craig splits up the crew. Why?"

Squid leaned down, and gave me a light kiss. "I hope we're paired."

I watched him while he opened his room. He looked back, gave me a smile, and then turned away. Freaky. I shook my head. I knew exactly what'd happened, and I didn't like it. I wanted no personal relationships on this tour. I needed to concentrate on my future with the ESF, with no distractions.

In my room, I threw my com and papers on my desk, and then poured a glass of wine—anything for some sleep tonight.

Why had Squid's action bothered me so much? I'd been kissed before—nothing new. Then Tyne popped into my mind, and I recognized who I really wanted to distract me.

Chapter Ten

connecting space
relinquishing
state of being

I rambled through the galley looking for food and caffeine. Grabbing a chair at a table where Mist and Tyne sat, I started on my tea.

No one spoke for a few moments. Then I asked, "What do you think we're going to find today? More tablets? They seem to be everywhere on Needles."

"*curious tablets,*
environment,
intriguing world," said Tyne.

He had that right, and then I realized I must be acclimatizing to his kaiku. I had actually understood Tyne's words. Now, I needed to work on understanding Keeki culture.

Major Craig dropped into a seat at our table. "How is everyone doing today?" She studied our faces. "Mist? Any problems, any concerns?"

She stared at Major Craig, and then said, "*irtl.*"

"Mist, you'll have to expand your explanation. Our translators don't know that word," said Major Craig. An extremely diplomatic comment from my mother.

This situation didn't happen often. Our translator implants usually exceeded my expectations. The kaiku did continue to stump us fairly often, though.

Mist threw a glance at Tyne; we all knew his explanations usually cleared up any ambiguities.

However, in this instance, Tyne, being the best Keeki interpreter we had, hesitated for a stretch of time.

Finally, Tyne said,

"*space to connect,*

relinquishing,
state of being."

"You need someplace to meditate?" asked a confused Major Craig, after a moment's thought. "We don't have many quiet areas, I agree."

I interrupted. "No, no, Mo…, Major Craig. I think Tyne means they need a place to connect with their religion, like a chapel." I'd almost called her Mom!

"Tyne, is Mile correct?" she asked, after giving me a glance of rebuke.

"Agreed," he answered. He studied me, perhaps considering my awkward interpretation.

"Okay, now I understand, Tyne. Good work, Mile. I'll find a small area for the Keeki to use. I'll work on our problem later today. We soon need to get going on our day."

Tyne continued to study me. He'd seemed happy about my interpretation of his kaiku. What bothered him?

"Anybody else have any concerns?" asked Major Craig.

Tyne didn't respond, and I shrugged, so we continued to eat with few words spoken. After swallowing her last bite, Major Craig stood and said in a voice loud enough to include everyone in the break room, "When we get to the ocean, we're going to split into three teams—one team of two divers to investigate the depths of the ocean, and two land teams. Mile, Tyne, and Mist: you'll be on one land team; Squid, Cam, and myself on the other. Major White and Briny will compose the ocean team. Any questions?"

I heard no protests, so I assumed the participants agreed with her arrangements. We packed up and left on the rover. After a short trip, we arrived at the ocean.

No intruding land masses broke the sparkling, deep blue sea. The airspace over the ocean was devoid of sea birds, and no fish leaped out of the water. I needed a look at some of Major White's maps and videos to understand this stretch of ocean.

Directly in front of us, the ocean had deposited a beach. Not a sparkling white, but more of a sparkling gray with other colors hinted at.

About thirty feet back from the ocean the edge of a forest followed the outline of the beach.

“Be back in three hours,” said Major Craig, “and we’ll debrief over lunch.”

Tyne, Mist, and I took off in one direction, while Mom, Squid, and Cam took off in another. I glanced back—Major White and Briny started to don their diving gear.

The three of us hugged the forest walking on a mossy area between the trees and the beach. The moss struck me as being similar to what I would’ve found on Earth, but of a browner hue. I studied the tree leaves and noticed different shapes and colors from our previous encounters. These leaves had a fairly round shape, and the colors tended towards green—much like Earth.

Silent Keeki unnerved me a bit, so I decided to engage them in conversation, as difficult as that could sometimes be. “What do the trees on Keeki look like?”

Mist glanced at Tyne, as if to say, *she’s all yours*. So Tyne said,

“*leaves of blue,*

tall,

trunks of brown.”

So, tall brown trees with blue leaves. Kind of matched their scales. “Did your ancestors fly to the tree tops? Did you have homes up there?”

Both heads swiveled in my direction. “I know you used to have wings, and fly about. The information was in our briefing back on Earth.”

“*long ago,*

changes,

unusual evolution happenings,” said Tyne.

“Yes, evolution does change things, doesn’t it? Actually, a precursor of human life began in our oceans. And that happened a long, long time ago. So did your ancestors land on your trees?” Tyne’s kaiku offered little content so I persisted.

“*top landings,*

vegetation,

nests in trees.”

Thoughts thudded my mind. “Do you still nest in trees?” I had no idea about their sex lives, and a curious teenager needed information.

“No,” said Mist. Tyne said nothing.

I suspected I’d reached the limits of useful Keeki information for today.

The ground beneath our feet allowed for a comfortable walk. As we strolled, the mossy area expanded while the forest retreated. Different types of vegetation emerged close to the forest's edge. Flowers caught my attention.

After a moment, Tyne and Mist started trotting after me. I bent down for a closer look at the flowers. Tyne grabbed my arm, and pulled me upwards.

"What're you doing?" I asked. "Let go." He had a strong grip, and my arm hurt.

"Poison," he commented. "Too close."

Again, another rash move on my part. "Maybe, but I'm more likely to have something happen to me when we're in an enclosed place, and not in nature—if you remember."

We had a staring match, for a couple of moments.

I gave in first. "Well, let's at least take cuttings. Maybe we can find foodstuffs to supplement our diet." I grabbed gloves and equipment.

After we took samples, we returned to the path. Soon the ocean shoreline took a sharp turn to our left. Rounding the corner, we now traversed a narrow bay with a tiny beach at its head.

As we walked from the mouth of the bay towards the beach, our path widened.

Then we made a discovery. Ruins nestled amongst the trees lining the beach caught our attention. Our ambling speeded up.

We carefully eased into the forest. As we began our investigation, we all pulled out our coms and took pictures. For about half an hour we wandered amongst the ruins that lined the head of the bay.

"What do you think we have here?" I asked. Before Tyne and Mist had a chance to respond, I said, "Personally, I think it's the remains of a village. These crumbling ruins look like foundations. Trees were probably used to build the walls and roof."

"*ancient civilization,*
disappeared,
Needles no longer," said Tyne.

I couldn't argue with his logic. The remnants appeared ancient, and skeletal remains continued to be elusive. "Time to get going, if we're to make our lunch rendezvous," I said.

We arrived at our starting point on time. As we settled on the grass to begin a lunch break, the other two away teams showed up.

With much laughter, the three teams relaxed.

"Mist, tell me what your team found," said Major Craig, after giving us time to unwind.

Mist discussed our samples taken, and the ruins discovered. "You guys are amazing. You're always finding something new," said Sylone. "I look forward to investigating this village. Tyne, Mist, Mile, please send your pictures to everyone, and give Cam your samples."

Major Craig continued, "Well, our group didn't find any exciting ruins, but we managed to discover unique vegetation—kind of like succulents, but with mostly purple coloring. Pictures will follow."

"Major White?" asked Mom.

Major White and Briny grinned at each other. "I believe you'll be pleased with our discoveries," said John. Then neither spoke.

What teases! An unusual response from the two of them.

"Give it up, Major," said Major Craig.

He laughed. "Okay. Our diving revealed lots of underwater shells and items similar to corals. Not much marine life; only tiny fish. Nothing to suggest they'd shed the shells we found."

Major White and Briny continued to smile. Actually, not smiles—wide grins.

"So, what's the big secret?" I couldn't hold my tongue.

Briny laughed. "We found another chest; possibly filled with tablets."

Another chest? "Where is it?" I practically yelled my words.

"Mile, calm," said my mother. Two words she'd often used during my informative years. "Although I have empathy for Mile's excitement and your presentation obviously encouraged her enthusiasm, please answer her question."

Major White replied, "The chest is still on the bottom of the ocean. We tried to lift it, but the weight was too much for both of us. I suggest we go back and open the container underwater, and then remove the contents in small quantities. The chest will then most likely be able to be lifted. Since it's underwater, I don't imagine it's filled with gas. Even if so, an underwater opening will let any gases disperse."

For some reason, I felt everyone looking my way.

"The chest is only in about five feet of water, so Major White and I can dig out the contents and give them to others to take to shore," said Briny, attempting to take everyone's attention away from me.

"An excellent plan," said Major Craig. "We'll all go after lunch."

Excitement grew amongst our crew—we had another chest to investigate.

"Major Craig, why was this particular ocean spot chosen for our investigations?" I asked. "I know we had a pointer that indicated we needed to go to the ocean, but why this spot?"

"Good question, Cadet Carter," said my mother, with a pleased look on her face. I tried to figure out why she was so pleased—although getting her approval did massage my ego—and then I realized I was the first to ask the question.

"Believe it or not," replied Major Craig, "Major White discovered, from orbit, an arrow-like rock formation pointing in this direction. So we went with the flow."

Mom laughed. "Okay, I know a lot of people donned their bathing suits this morning, so let's get going," said Major Craig. "Anyone not want to get into the water and retrieve stuff?"

The Keeki looked at each other.

"*top water,*

life,

place only possible," said Aran.

Mountains and now water? What else didn't I understand about our comrades?

Major Craig studied Aran and the other Keeki. "So you'll only be on water, like in a boat, and not in it? Is this correct?"

"*flying species,*

descendants,

drown in water," said Tyne.

"I don't imagine that's still true," said Major Craig, "however, I'll let it go." She glanced around, "Okay, everyone else, let's start this party."

I interrupted. "Major Craig, I'd like to stay on shore and search for pebbles, shells, and such. May I join the Keeki?"

She smiled. "Not a bad idea. We all know what you like to collect, and there're plenty of us to retrieve…whatever we're going to retrieve."

So I stayed behind with the Keeki, and collected trinkets. I actually had a great time—even Aran seemed to enjoy looking for objects in the sand. A bird-like trait, perhaps?

As the contents of the chest were dumped on the beach, I caught a glimpse of Major White and Briny leaving to explore other areas along the coast line. The first chest was not deep enough to require diving gear, so John and Briny had left the recovery to us, and taken off to continue their adventure.

"My goodness," I said, after I examined the pile of artifacts on the shore, "that must be one large chest."

Major Craig laughed. "Yes." She pointed out to sea. Four humans tried to drag the chest in question to shore.

Much bigger than the previous ones, I wondered what markings the outside held. In the meantime, I decided to study the contents of the chest, and ignore the commotion around me.

"Mile, you're not paying attention," said Cam, touching my shoulder.

"What?" I glanced up. Why was he bothering me? He knew we had a lot to study.

"Major White and Briny are yelling from a ways down the beach."

"What about? Are they in trouble?" My pulse quickened.

"No, not at all. They've found another artifact." Cam grinned.

"Really? Well, let's go. What're you standing there for?" We raced down the sand, along with everyone else.

A round, brown, stone-like container about a foot and a half in diameter, with a tall pole perched on the artifact's lid caught our attention. A circling, sparkling sun catcher topped the pole. The artifact had been dragged onto the beach by Major White and Briny, while the rest of us gathered.

"How did you find this?" I asked the grinning pair.

"The top stuck out of the water. We figured the location was about eight feet deep, so we dove in," said Briny. "I thought it might have been the top of a tree, or perhaps a mast from a sunken boat—which would have been exciting."

"Our day for artifacts," said a pleased Major White.

"Sure looks like an arrow on top," Squid commented. "We were meant to find this."

"You may be right." Major Craig looked at Briny. "This is just as exciting as any old sunken ship. So, let's get back to the lab and open it up. Cam?"

"Certainly. We have puzzles to solve from the first chest we found today, and we'll soon find out what's in this one."

Our enthusiasm let us accomplish our packing up in record time.

Back at the ship, I helped Cam and Briny sample the artifacts we'd found today. Then I watched Cam open the round object under his fume hood.

We found round tablets inside covered in markings. No other items existed in the container.

We were all distracted at dinner as we received the oodles of pictures from today's excursion. The numerous writings, or should I say characters, surfacing on the artifacts, pyramid walls, and such, overwhelmed me. Would I be able to find some link between them?

Major White and Cam decided to return to the bridge to make another survey of Needles. They needed to determine any signals, landmarks, or pointers had missed their scrutiny. Today's *arrow* worried them.

Major Craig disappeared while we continued our investigations. When she returned, she announced, "Earth has responded to my previous messages. They've found that all tablets point to a new location. A new location in space, I should say. Although I don't know how they figured that out." Sylone studied our faces for a moment. Apparently, she liked what she saw because she said, "We've been ordered to travel to these new coordinates and investigate. Any objections? Not that it'd do you any good, of course, but I'd like to know your thoughts."

Laughter circled the break room. "How long is the journey?" I asked.

"About three days. The coordinates point to another planet."

"Do we know anything about this new world?" I asked.

"No, we only have a location. The translation did say it was a planet, though." Major Craig studied the crowd. "I'm going to send everyone the transmission I received from Earth. The missive includes their translations of the first artifacts. Perhaps it'll help us translate our new puzzles."

After the conversational buzz died, the majority of us settled down for some serious puzzle solving.

Soon my subconscious received the impression of arguing. My senses returned to the real world and I realized Tyne and Squid glowered at each other. By now I knew enough about both of them to recognize a few of their moods.

"What's going on?" My mind had a hard time focusing on this new topic.

"Nothing," said Squid.

"Disagreement," answered Tyne.

Disagreement about nothing? Not likely. However, being a wise eighteen-year-old, I changed the subject. But I really did wonder what their conflict, or at least the underlying emotions, was all about.

Chapter Eleven

cadet surprise
unknown
wonders to behold

I settled down and took a look at the photos from the first chest discovered today. The images reminded me of the ones inside the pyramid, so I decided to make a comparison.

With my mind semi-occupied, I asked, "What do you guys think we'll discover at this new planet?" I waited for an answer, but no one spoke. "Tyne, have the Keeki been there before?" Still suspicious of the Keeki because of the information they'd hidden about Needles, nonetheless I tried to be tactful.

"*cadet surprise,*
unknown,
wonders to behold."

I studied the Keeki. From what I could analyze, Tyne admitted to knowing nothing about this new planet, but he didn't rule out Aran having knowledge. My attention would remain on the Keeki leader.

We soon gave up puzzling and retired for an early night.

****

The trip to the new planet resulted in a number of cranky people. We were all used to exploring outside the ship every day, and the Keeki's claustrophobia came back to haunt them. They spent a great deal of time in the break room—the largest room on *Skyfall*.

Most of us had been assigned a short course to study—at least for the humans. Mine involved first contact procedures. I suspected Mom wanted me to be more comfortable with alien species, if and when we came into contact with others. Of course, I may have been doing her a disservice—perhaps all humans received the same course. I decided not to ask the Keeki if they were studying anything. I probably wouldn't have understood their kaiku anyway.

When the rules of first contact didn't occupy my time, I painted and puzzled on the artifacts we'd discovered.

On the morning of the third day, I heard a slight commotion and noticed all Keeki entering the break room. Too engrossed in painting, I hadn't noticed they'd all disappeared.

Tyne carried his painting supplies and sat beside me.

"Painting?" he asked.

"Yes. A good day; much has been accomplished. How about you?" I pointed at his paint box. "Are you going to be creative, too?"

He took a small blank box out of a pocket.

"*paint design,*
creating,
gift to present."

So some lucky person will receive a piece of Tyne's art.

"Where did all the Keeki go? Did you have a meeting?" I hoped my question didn't involve some Keeki hidden ritual.

"*irtl.*"

Oh, the chapel. Mom must have found an area for the Keeki to use for their religious meetings.

Before I satisfied my curiosity with questions, Tyne said,
"*found space,*
empty,
cabin of irtl."

That's right we did have an empty cabin.

I couldn't summon the nerve to ask if a non-Keeki could watch one of their services, or whatever they did in their *irtl*, so I went back to my painting and calmed my breathing.

"Look out the viewport," announced Major White over the intercom, distracting me from my thoughts. I raced over and pulled the shutters of the break room window aside.

A world covered with water drew my attention.

"Agora," said Mist, from over my shoulder, startling me.

"What do you mean? What does Agora mean?" I asked.

"*moisture abundance,*
flowing,
world of water," said Tyne.

Okay, this time Tyne confused me just as much as Mist, so I asked, "Agora is a name?"

Mist nodded.

"We might want to check with Major Craig, but Agora seems like a good name for this world. Quite catchy, Mist," I said.

"Better than what Earth wants to call it," said Major Craig, surprising us. She'd quietly entered the break room during our discussion.

I gave her a questioning look.

"Oh, some combination of letters and numbers—the usual bureaucratic nightmare."

"When will we get there? Where should we start exploring?" I wanted to start running around the room—another planet to dig into!

"First decision, the planet is called Agora. At least, unofficially," said Major Craig, "since I've heard no objections."

Mist sported a slight smile. I suspected her shyness often limited her words, but my mother's decision obviously pleased her.

"We'll be there in about three hours, and Major White knows where we should start exploring." Her comment silenced the break room.

"How does he know?" asked Squid, always the skeptical one.

Major Craig laughed. "Apparently, he discovered a satellite orbiting Agora and we're receiving a message with coordinates."

Kind of spooky, I thought.

"So what's the plan?" I asked.

"We're going to land *Starfly* near the site indicated by the satellite. Since we'll arrive midafternoon, we'll send out three away teams to study the area around the ship. Just a short foray. Then we'll return and discuss our findings and formulate tomorrow's plans. Any questions?"

Her suggestion sounded fine to everyone, so we cleaned up. Hobbies and study materials scattered throughout the break room for the last three days definitely needed to disappear, and our cabins got makeovers. After a substantive meal, Major Craig organized the teams, and we supplied our packs. Then we gathered in the break room to await our arrival. The landing seemed a bit anticlimactic for some reason. Perhaps landings had become commonplace—although a little egotistical to think of myself as a sophisticated astronaut.

After Cam gave his okay, we gathered outside the ship and breathed in the atmosphere. Our landing spot consisted of a flat area close to an ocean beach. Before we landed, Major White sent everyone pictures of three continents, and a great deal of blue-green ocean. The coordinates from the satellite pointed to a place on the continent shaped like South America.

Aran, Tyne, and I walked towards the beach. Our team's assignment was to study the coast line. Our mission was to walk in one direction for an hour, and then take samples as we returned to the ship. Daylight wouldn't last much longer than three hours, so Major Craig wanted everyone ensconced in the ship before nightfall. She sent a security personnel along with each team because of our lack of knowledge about this planet.

The beach of sparkling sand reached in both directions. I immediately bent down to examine the wonders before me.

Tyne yanked me up. "Will you stop doing that?" I asked. A little too physical for me lately, I needed to have a talk with him.

"Poison," he said, studying my face.

"I'm not going to be poisoned by sand. It's not like I'm trying to sniff flowers or anything. I just wanted to see if this planet had any of my shiny stones." Actually, my pronouncement lacked credibility—I had no idea what could hide in the shoreline?

Tyne didn't respond verbally, but he did let go of my arm. "Okay, okay. I'll look for stuff later. Let's get walking, then," I said.

We walked north—at least, what I wanted to call north. The ocean on our left was offset by a cliff area on our right.

I tried to ignore the lure of the beach front, and concentrate on the cliffs. They started off at ten feet and gradually rose to about thirty feet and then appeared to level off. No evidence of erosion on the dull, beige surfaces exposed to us was evident, and I suspected a plateau existed on the cliff tops. However, I didn't think Major Craig meant for our team to go off on a side trip to investigate, so I needed to content myself with putting recommendations in my report.

After a short time, we happened upon ruins. Although, with a closer look, the structure's age didn't qualify as ancient, so we needed a better description than ruins.

I decided we had a terrace with eight landings. Because of their consistent dimensions, they were obviously manufactured. By whom, I didn't know. Inhabitants? Visiting aliens?

Our away team was thunderstruck by the object's strange nature. After each ocean wave hit, water flowed down the terraces and sounds played upon the air, so I listened for a pattern.

"What's this?" I asked. "Why're we hearing music? *Is this music?*" The tones seemed like musical notes, but I was far from being an expert.

“*subjective feelings,*
similar,
Keeki musical compositions,” said Tyne.

“So you think we’re hearing music. Interesting. How’s it produced?”

“*water flowing,*
gyra,
channels of constriction,” said Tyne.

I sort of understood that *channels of constrictions* produced various sounds. *Gyra* eluded me.

“So you think this is like an organ, but with water instead of air making the sounds?”

Tyne made a motion of agreement.

“Okay, why don’t we circle around this organ structure, and see what else we can find.”

We wandered until we came to striations etched on the wall. I peered closer and recognized something familiar.

“Puzzle!” yelled Tyne. Quite a surprise since Tyne didn’t normally raise his voice.

“What do you mean?” I needed to keep a close eye on his mood.

“Numbers,” said Tyne, pointing to the markings, “puzzle shape.”

I studied the wall. Aran interrupted my musings, “Nonogram. Similar.”

Although he’d never stuck around in the evenings, he somehow recognized our evening puzzling.

Nonetheless, I said, “Sure does look like a nonogram. Let’s take lots of pictures, and we can study the puzzle later.”

Aran seemed a little put out by my pronouncement—probably something to do with his being the leader of this away team. Oh, well. If nothing else, I expected a reprimand. So I waited for Aran to suggest our next action.

He caught my hint. “Continue.”

I followed Tyne and Aran since my interpretation of Aran’s one word indicated to me we needed to investigate the remaining sides of this musical instrument.

We wandered around the structure. Two repetitions of the nonogram occurred, but nothing else of interest.

“Climb,” said Aran.

We scampered to the top.

The first side we stopped at dropped directly to the water. The beach had disappeared, and the side of the ruin plunged into the ocean.

"I'm going to take pictures. We need to get a better idea of the surrounding area," I said. Tyne walked away to study the top of the organ.

When I came upon the second side, I discovered wondrous ruins. "Aran, Tyne, look over here."

They rushed over to my position. Ruins, reminding me of foundations, covered the ground below us. A small village? Perhaps for a congregation that built the ocean organ to enjoy their love of music?

"Pictures," said Aran, "analyze on ship."

Okay, I could live with his instruction. After memorializing the area, Aran said, "Ocean discovery."

I imagined he meant we should go to the other side of the ocean organ's top and see what we could discover about the water. Apparently, the Keeki loved water—in strange ways.

Aran hovered beside me after we arrived, which struck me as strange. He usually stuck to any Keeki around.

I looked down and tried to figure out how the organ fit into the rest of the ruins on Needles. Maybe this was one of their creative outlets?

Much to my surprise, I flew off the cliff.

Chapter Twelve

underwater death
concerning
drowning of human

After I spat out way too much ocean and had a moment to think, I decided my surroundings had quite a nice temperature and a palatable taste, I hoped. Awkwardly, while treading water, I pulled off my coveralls to uncover my swim suit. Pretty sure I'd been the first to partake in the waters of Agora, I suspected a great number of comments to come my way.

Deep enough for swimming, I held my coveralls and tools in one hand and pedaled slowly on my back to the shoreline. Not that there was much of a beach—the top of the ruins, at this point, dropped almost directly into the ocean. So I angled my path towards the edge of the ruins to find a landing spot.

"Mile!" Tyne yelled.

The shore neared, so I said, "I'm okay. I'll be there in a minute." Tyne and the security guard pulled me out when I arrived.

Tyne grabbed my shoulders and said,

"*underwater death,*
concerning,
drowning of human."

What did Tyne's kaiku mean? Then I understood. "Tyne, I know how to swim, I wouldn't have died. I wore my swimsuit today, so I just needed to take off my overalls because they were too constricting for swimming."

Tyne and Aran studied my body. Frankly, their gazes made me uncomfortable, especially Aran. On the other hand, Tyne's interest intrigued me.

"Tyne, I'm fine. If you want to go for a swim, just let me know. I love being in the water. Water sports not so much, but swimming and floating about is delightful."

Tyne dropped his hands from my shoulders, and said, "Keeki, not *in* water."

No kaiku words, but I understood. "Why not?"

"*historical death,*

beneath,

safe on water."

Historical death? "Do you mean your ancestors couldn't swim?" Best I could come up with whilst dripping wet.

"Evolution," said Tyne.

I thought perhaps I'd heard agreement. "Okay. Well, I need to get back to the ship. The air temperature's not bad right now, but I can feel it dropping. I need to get some dry clothes."

Our time to return was imminent anyways. We sped up our pace so we got back in less than an hour. I ran to my room and had a quick shower. With my disposition much improved I graced the break room.

After eating like people who hadn't eaten for days, the away teams made their reports.

The other two teams had explored the areas to the south and east.

The south team followed the shoreline for ninety minutes and then turned back and followed the base of the plateau. Their report didn't contradict or add anything to what our team had discovered.

The east team got a bit more exercise than the other two teams—they climbed up to the flat top of the plateau and got a great view of the area opposite the ocean. Two major features were a large blue-green tinted lake and a orange-hued forest—areas for future exploration.

The ocean organ elicited great interest. A discussion of music erupted, but Major Craig refocused our thoughts.

Then enthusiasm burst forth again when we sent everyone pictures of the nonogram found on the side of the organ's walls.

Of course, Mom put up an alarm about my dip in the ocean. "You need blood tests. Briny, please check Mile for any possible contamination."

I started to protest, but then I saw the look on Mom's face. Since Briny declined to interrupt our staring match, I decided to reign in my objections.

"Now that I've heard all the verbal reports, it's time for everyone to do write ups." No mutters; just our regular procedure, after all.

"Cadet Carter, I want to talk to you. Please join me." Mom stood and walked away. I had little choice but to follow.

After we settled in the tiny office attached to her cabin, she asked, "Are you really okay?" I nodded. "Tell me what really happened. How did you manage to fall off the cliff?"

Mom had gotten to the crux of the matter. "I don't really know. Tyne, Aran, and I were looking around the surrounding area, and I went quite close to the edge of the ocean organ's top. I wanted to see if any islands were within our reach or if any existed, actually. I felt a tiny bump, and the next thing I knew I flew through the air—just a little bit of cliff diving, really."

My dear mother was not amused by my attempt at humor. "Were you pushed?" she asked.

Good question. "The closest person was Aran—actually right behind me. Tyne was traipsing around the top, and I was kind of ignoring him. I thought I felt a tap, but I was concentrating on the view, so I didn't really pay a lot of attention to the other two."

"Do you have any reason to suspect Aran?" she asked, after a moment's thought.

Another good question. "I don't really trust him. He seems to have the Keeki foremost in his thoughts. Understandable I guess, but he gives me the wrong vibes."

Major Craig, my only mother, gave me the longest look. "Keep a close watch on everyone around you. I'd like my daughter to survive her first away mission." She stood and gathered me in her embrace. "I know I haven't been very accessible to you, darling Mileena, but it's difficult keeping our secret. If you need to talk, just let me know. My door is always open."

I tried not to grin.

"Okay, where did that smirk come from?" she asked, a trifle annoyed.

"Well, I know I shouldn't say this, but I'm sure Major White appreciates your open door." I burst out in giggles. After a shocked glance at me, my mother started laughing too. We hugged again, and she asked, "Does our relationship bother you?"

"Not at all. You need *friends.* I've just had a hard time keeping my mouth shut." With no clue how she'd take my statement about *friends*, I stopped talking.

We looked at each other for a long moment, then we both giggled—we had the same sense of humor. After a final embrace, she sent me on my way.

At least, there had been no questions about *my* love life.

After a visit to Briny in the med lab for blood tests regarding my dump in the ocean, I went to the break room and settled at Mist's table. "I need to ask you something about the Keeki. Is that okay?" I hoped Mist was receptive. Some days she seemed resentful of my presence.

"Agreed."

Not much of answer but I figured she gave me the go-ahead. "How do I remove Tyne's painting from my hand?"

"Why?" Mist's voice took a drop in tone bringing to mind a wind chill.

Good question. "Ah, I've had negative comments from some humans." Actually, harassment, but I didn't want to explain that concept.

"Special fluid," said Mist. "Join."

So the two of us went to Mist's stateroom. Quite an interesting room. Her walls were covered with pictures, all done in shades of red and orange. Mist gave me a bottle filled with a liquid, and then we returned to the break room. We hadn't spoken during the entire encounter.

I sat down at Tyne's table, and Mist returned to hers. Tyne pointed at the bottle in my hand. "What?" he asked.

Oh, oh. How do I explain this? "Let's go outside, for a moment," I suggested. Tyne didn't argue with my request. All I saw were a couple of the security staff tossing a ball around.

Tyne studied my face, after we stopped walking. "Explain," he said, indicating the bottle still in my hand.

I sighed. "I've received nasty comments about the design. Don't get me wrong, I really love your painting, but I wanted to have the design removed so no one would notice my hand. I really think you're quite an artist, Tyne."

Tyne reached out with his hand and touched my cheek, and then stroked it a second time. And then he rubbed my painted hand.

"*denotation declaration,*
consideration,
of future feelings."

Mist might need to explain Tyne's words, but I thought I had a pretty good idea of Tyne's mood.

"*unreasonable responses,*
confrontation,
regarding art forms."

"No, no. There's no need for you to talk to anyone, Tyne. I'll deal with the situation." This kaiku I understood.

His hand crept out to touch my ear.

A blissful moment enveloped me until I realized Tyne's stroking my ear had created an emotional reaction. Did his action bother me? I took a deep breath—in more ways than one, I decided.

Ignoring my thoughts and feelings, I asked, "Perhaps you'd like to draw on my skin some other place. On my upper back?" I pulled my coveralls down a bit from my hairline and pointed to the obvious body part.

His hand crept up and touched my skin. "Yes."

My body started to respond to his nearness. "Ah, we'll have to find a time and a bit of privacy so you can do your painting. In the meantime, I think we should go back and work on some puzzles."

I tried to calm my breathing. Silence enveloped our walk.

Tyne and I sat down with Mist and Squid in the break room and got out our coms. I, for one, needed to decide what I wanted to work on in order to ignore the situation I'd just run away from.

Looking at the pyramids on my tiny screen, I asked, "Do the Keeki have structures like the pyramids we discovered?"

Mist and Tyne glanced at each other, and then Tyne said,

"*worship place,*
expressing,
concepts of religion."

The words took me a minute, but then I thought I understood. "Pyramids are churches on Keeki? Or, I guess I should ask if churches look like pyramids on Keeki?"

Tyne made a positive motion with his hand. "*irtl.*"

The stateroom Mom had found for their church certainly wasn't a pyramid, but Tyne seemed to have just confirmed what their *irtls* looked like.

I decided my understanding of Keeki language and customs had begun to develop quite nicely. "Do you have more than one type of church? Does everyone worship in these churches? What colors are predominant? What kind of religion, or religions do you have? What are their basic tenants?" I babbled, but I really wanted to understand the Keeki.

"*emotions erupt,*
coloring,
red and orange," replied Mist.

Red and orange? Emotions? Then I took a leap. "Mist, you have pictures on your walls in your cabin. They're predominantly red and orange. Are they religious drawings?"

Mist made a head motion I understood as agreement.

Interesting. Perhaps Mist was devotedly religious? "How about my other questions? Would anyone like to comment?"

Mist said, "Hard to discuss. Send information."

"Excellent idea." I could live with receiving the information in a text form—certainly easier than deciphering their kaiku. At least, I could study her information in private, rather than both of us being on the spot and required to respond.

During our entire conversation, Squid said nothing but studied Mist and her words. "Mile, using the information you cracked inside the pyramids, I'm going to tackle this nonogram you guys discovered today on the ocean organ," said Squid. "I think its solution may involve the dictionary you unearthed."

Squid's concept interested me, so I decided to echo him. We all settled down to our own projects. Not sure what Mist and Tyne worked on, but I understood where Squid and I focused.

The pictures taken today interested me. Squid was quite correct the ocean organ nonogram markings appeared to be related to my dictionary, so I focused my solving according to Squid's thoughts.

Squid jumped up, "I've got it! Woo, hoo!"

Silence enveloped the break room. "What do you mean?" asked Major White.

"I've figured out the ocean organ nonogram." Squid beamed.

"You'd best give us a hint," I suggested.

"Yeah, yeah. Okay, I used Mile's translation of the dictionary to put numbers on the two sides of the nonogram. After it all worked out—really wasn't that hard—I realized the drawing I'd uncovered actually included numbers from her dictionary. Then I translated those numbers back to human ones. See?" Squid pointed at his piece of paper. "I think this might be a set of coordinates," he continued.

Squid's words caught Major White's and Cam's attention. They peered over his shoulder, and conferred.

"I think you've found a latitude and longitude," agreed Cam.

Latitude and longitude? "Can you relate these numbers to a position on Agora?" I asked.

"Ah," said Major White, "that's what computers are for. Squid, help Cam and me figure out something for our nav computer to do. You might want to send everyone your solution first, though."

Major White, Cam, and Squid left the break room, with Squid grinning from ear to ear.

I studied his solution. The squiggles seemed to resemble a set of numbers—at least according to *my* dictionary.

I thought about my dictionary. Having one of my ideas prove useful delighted me. Hopefully, my interpretations were correct. If Squid's coordinates led us to another interesting site, my future involved a happy dance.

Then I thought about Tyne, and his religions, and his dancing, and his touches on my skin.

Where was our relationship going? Where…?

Cam and Squid's return interrupted my musings. "Any location?" I asked.

"Oh, yes. Major White is telling Major Craig as we speak." Squid had a pleased glow.

"A location near here?" I asked.

"Pretty close," said Cam. "As long as our computer program was right, of course. And if it wasn't, we'll take another look. The algorithm seemed pretty tight, though."

His comment confused me, but I didn't want to appear negative. "Squid, that was pretty quick work on the nonogram. I think you really like working on them."

"Oh, I do. They're fascinating."

"So where's this new location?" I asked.

"Let's wait until John and Sylone return," said Cam. "The decision is theirs."

Chapter Thirteen

watching Keeki
lingering
outside aroma smell

I tried to settle down to puzzle, but my mind wouldn't focus. Thankfully, the majors didn't take long to return.

"Well, sure looks like you smart guys found a new location for us to explore," said Sylone.

Although vague as to whom she referred to as being smart—those of us who found the nonogram, or Squid who deciphered it, or whoever wrote the computer program—I basked in the glory, anyway.

"Do we know what's at the coordinates?" I asked. A bit of a silly question, but I couldn't help myself.

"The only thing we know is that the location is close to the ocean at the northernmost point of this continent. While we do need further study of our current location, we'll go to the new coordinates tomorrow. We can always come back, and the idea of being pointed to a location intrigues me." Mom paused, for a moment. "Of course, we may be entirely wrong with our interpretation of the coordinates. If so, heads will fall."

Much laughter ensued.

"Anyway, I'm off. Earth needs to know about what we've found, and I have innumerable reports to write." She glanced around the break room before she left.

I suspected she wanted to say *have an early night* but resisted.

We settled back into puzzling. Squid's solution had spurred a number of people to try and figure out some of our remaining problems. I also suspected fiendish nonograms would pop up for our next competition.

Tyne and Mist made an evening disappearance, and not for the first time. Glancing around the break room, I hoped to also make a quiet departure.

After I went through the doorway leading to the outside, I was stopped by a security guard. We're guarding the ship?

"Where're you going, Mile?" asked the security guy. No unknown identities on this expedition.

"Actually, Simon, I'm looking for Tyne and Mist. Why are you here?"

"Major White wants advance notice of any fauna sniffing around. Standard procedure," replied Simon. "Security covers this entrance twenty-four /seven."

"Hmm, good plan. Do you know where Tyne and Mist went?" I asked.

"There's a flat area on the other side." Simon pointed towards the nose of our spaceship.

"Okay, thanks. I'm going to find them. Don't tell anyone I was here."

Simon gave me a disgusted look and shook his head as he entered my exit from the ship in his log book. "I won't volunteer the information, Mile. Otherwise, you're on your own." He shook his head again.

I should have remembered about security protocols—all those courses at ESF should have clued me in?

I walked around the nose of the ship, and found Tyne and Mist and the other Keeki. I backed up and tried to stay out of sight while I studied their actions.

With their arms spread wide, the Keeki executed a kind of dance. Their expedition overalls had been removed, but they still wore their Keeki under garments. Their underwear had wide underarm slits but, otherwise, reminded me of one piece shorts/sleeveless-top combos.

Their iridescent vestigial wings showed under their arms. However, their dancing interested me more. Were they dancing together? Or did they each express *something* I had no clue about?

I watched for a while, and when they stopped to take a rest, I decided to disappear before they discovered my presence.

****

At breakfast the next morning, Tyne and Mist sat down at my table. I'd hoped for a quiet moment to consider a few topics but, apparently, breakfast would not be the time.

"*watching Keeki,*
lingering,
outside aroma smell?" asked Tyne.

Oh, so they'd smelled me even though I'd tried to stay out of sight behind the ship. *Now, what do I say?* "I was out for a walk but didn't want to interrupt your, ah, whatever it was, so I tried to stay hidden and not bother you." A slight lie, but not one that bothered me.

Tyne and Mist didn't respond, so I jumped in. "What were you doing?" I asked. "Your actions seemed very dancelike."

Mist sniffed and said, "Upset." She left the break room without another word.

"What's wrong with Mist?" I asked Tyne.

"*human smell,*
intruding,
dances honoring ancestors."

So my scent intruded, did it? Well, that was Mist's problem not mine. A thought popped into my mind, so I asked, "Does my smell bother you, Tyne?"

"Intriguing," he said, touching the top of my right hand with two of his fingers. He then startled me by grabbing hold of my hand with both of his.

"*shining eyes,*
intriguing,
skin of silk," he reiterated.

Tyne owned the words—even though their presentation was a little unusual. "I'd like to join you the next time you honor your ancestors. May I?" Then I thought about the other Keeki involved. "Maybe Mist wouldn't want me there?"

Tyne grunted. The sound reminded me of a human sigh.

"*female Keeki,*
disappointing,
human female reaction."

Now, what the hell did his kaiku mean? Was Tyne disappointed with Mist? Or maybe with me for not getting along with his compatriot?

"*behold dance,*
personal,
pleased to exist," said Tyne.

I gave Tyne a wide smile. My interpretation gave me a warm glow—he wanted to spend time with me, and Keeki time at that.

Major Craig interrupted my breakfast dreaming. "Okay, everyone. Get your packs and meet outside in ten minutes. We're taking the rover to our next location."

I ran to my room and threw together essentials. I think everyone was as excited as I was as our group reformed outside the ship in record time.

The rover drove close to the shoreline. The ground was flat and able to hold our vehicle's weight.

As we proceeded away from the ocean organ, the land began to change. More vegetation appeared, and the varieties began to increase in height. After an hour or so passed, we came upon the beginnings of a forest. Quite a healthy looking forest, by human standards.

"Do your forests look like this?" I asked Tyne, who sat beside me.

"*blue forests,*
existing,
flowers of yellow," he replied.

I guessed his answer was no. I had no idea what to ask next, so I fell silent. I needed to figure out ways to converse with aliens. My recent First Contact course needed improvement. Maybe I should write my own. Hmm…

"*silver tusks,*
meaning?
interspersed in forest," asked Tyne.

His question brought me out of my reverie. Silver tusks?

I glanced outside the rover, and figured out his confusion. "Tyne, those *husks* are fallen trees. They're dead now, so any greenery—life, I mean—has disappeared and that's why they look silvery."

Tyne made no response. Had he understood my explanation?

"I think the water level of the ocean has lowered," I said. "Look at the shoreline; it seems to be receding. There's a gap between the sand and the water. I guess what I'm trying to say is the sand has given away to ocean bottom."

"Receding?" asked Tyne.

Cam took this one. "For some reason, the ocean's water level has lowered. Perhaps global warming has been reversed, or perhaps some other explanation. I don't even know if this planet experienced global warming, or the natural progression of ice ages. We'll have to study the whole world to find some rudimentary understanding. We'll have to study fossil records, and…" Cam trailed off.

"*ocean water,*
lowering,
unknown on Keeki?" asked Tyne.

Cam shook his head. "I have no idea about your planet's ecosphere. And I certainly have no idea about Agora's. Earth has had its own issues, that's why we try to find familiar patterns. Maybe nothing is similar on Keeki."

No one had any words. So many planets; so many ecologies.

We parked beside a hillside. And, since it was within yards of our intended destination, we'd found a good place to stop our travels and have lunch.

I grabbed my lunch bag, studied my environment, and started walking.

"Mile?" asked Squid, stopping my progress.

"I figure I'll eat and walk. Should be healthy, right?" I needed quiet time.

Before I'd had one quiet thought, Tyne and Squid were at my side. "I need exercise, too," said Squid. "A good idea."

Well, I couldn't argue about exercise, so I didn't respond. We'd all been cooped up traveling to this new location, and my quiet time would have to wait.

"Where did your coordinates point to? Something around here?" I asked Squid.

He pecked at his com. "Actually, we're very close. Just over here." He walked towards the short hillside, and Tyne and I followed.

Glancing at the terrain, I said, "I'm going to sit down and finish my lunch." I plunked myself on the ground, and the boys followed. "We can look around and study the area while we do so. Don't forget to hydrate," I said.

Now I sounded like my mother but my idea had a basis in reality, and I heard no complaints.

While I munched my sandwich I studied the outer surface of the hill. The ocean's edge loomed nearby but, even so, the vegetation appeared dry.

Then I found two darker patches. I started waving my hand around. "Guys, look there, and there. What do you think those areas are?"

They both followed my waving hand, but said nothing. "Okay, someone give me your thoughts."

"Perhaps an entrance? Or a different kind of foliage?" suggested Squid.

"Explore," said Tyne, always the minimalist.

"Exactly." I looked around, and waved my arm. "Major Craig, please come over here." She had apparently decided walking and eating was a good idea, too, and was near to us.

"What is it, Mile?" she asked, wiping her mouth with a napkin.

I grinned. "We think those two dark spots are something to investigate. Maybe an underground passage."

Squid raised his arm, and started to protest. "I never said…"

Major Craig interrupted. "Don't worry, Squid. I'm sure Mile got carried away with her enthusiasm. Who knows what those dark patches mean? However, I do agree the two areas should be investigated. Good going."

Squid relaxed after her words of encouragement.

Sylone turned away, and gathered up the others. After everyone assembled, she said, "We have two areas to explore." She pointed to the two indicators and split up the crew. "Now, do a little investigating and then report back. Do not go any further than the outside surface of the hill."

Our group was sent to the dark area furthest from the ocean. We found nothing of any significance, but took samples anyway.

We returned to our meeting spot and found out the other crew had discovered a cave entrance. Major Craig announced, "Cam and Aran, I want you two to go into the cave and explore. Keep your com open so we can communicate on your progress."

Cam and Aran took off at a rapid rate. The rest of us settled down to wait—not very patiently, on my part.

We all scrunched together and listened to Major Craig's com as they proceeded down the cave. I had so many questions.

The two of them soon returned. Major Craig said, "I know you described the caves over the com as you explored but give a summary, in case we misunderstood anything."

Cam said, "The cave we entered was pretty dark and very dusty. We activated our headlamps and cautiously walked forward. The walls had little markings; at least what we could see with our dim lights. Soon we came to a crossroads. The path split into two branches, and that's when we decided to return. We need more manpower to properly explore the possibilities."

Chapter Fourteen

softness delight
exciting
pleasure all mine?

"Good analysis, Cam" said Major Craig. "So, we're going to split up into two groups—one for each branch of the path. Then we'll meet back at the junction in thirty minutes." Mom divvied up our personnel, and I landed on the same away team with her, along with Tyne and Squid.

We looked around the junction, collected samples, and then our team proceeded down our chosen passage way.

A bleak corridor greeted us. Our headlamps made the passage accessible and helped us easily focus on the dusty brown walls and gravelly floor.

I hung back a bit as the ceiling hovered far too close to my head, and made my steps hesitant.

Mom let Tyne and Squid go ahead while she dropped back to talk to me. "Everything okay?"

"I really don't like being underground, but I'll be alright." Trickles of sweat began to appear on various body parts.

"Ah, your claustrophobia is back, I see. I suspected as much—usually you're out ahead of everyone."

"I can do this," I mumbled.

"Of course you can. We'll be turning back shortly, as our time is almost up. The junction has a much higher ceiling; you'll be okay there."

My mother's statement perked me up.

We continuously took samples, but there wasn't any life—plant or otherwise—to be found. And then the passageway dead ended. Returning to our meeting place, we joined the other away team. A sense of relief came over me. The ceiling was high enough to let my feelings of being enclosed ease a little.

"Anything to report?" asked Mom of the other team.

Cam grinned. “Yes, we’ve found an artifact!” Pleasure graced his face.

“You might want to be a bit more detailed,” said my mother, exhibiting her dry sense of humor. I wished I could be so amusing.

“Right, right. The corridor we walked down was quite boring. We took samples, but found nothing of interest—at least on the surface. Testing may prove otherwise.” Cam thought for a moment, getting his thoughts in order, I assumed. “Then the path deposited us in a cavern. Quite a large area. Only estimating here but maybe thirty feet square? I’ll use my laser pointer next time to get a more accurate reading.” He grinned. Cam thought of himself as the great explorer.

“I still haven’t heard anything about an artifact,” commented my mother.

“Ah, right. Inside the cavern we found what looked like a shrine. Maybe. Not a very scientific analysis but we need further study. The rest of the cavern was pretty much empty. Benches were scattered about, so that’s why I called the artifact a shrine.”

“Any further items of interest?” asked Major Craig.

“Probably not, but we didn’t take a completely thorough look. I decided we’d better return and report. More eyes are needed.”

“Good decision. Okay, everyone. Grab your belongings, we’re going to see Cam’s team’s discovery.”

Cam’s comment about a shrine intrigued me. Would this be a religious artifact? Perhaps something the Keeki would understand, but would they know how to explain it to us? So many questions. I loved exploring—so much to add to my knowledge base.

We proceeded at a rapid pace down the second passageway. Readings and samples had already been taken, so nothing stopped us rushing to the artifact.

After we entered the cavern, my rough guess agreed with Cam’s estimates of its dimensions. He was also correct about only one visible artifact of any concern.

I inched forward to take a closer look at the shrine. With surfaces mainly red and gold and quite shiny, the markings on the top were obvious. I looked around the sides to complete my perusal. The front intrigued me the most because I thought I saw a small door.

Peering down, I flew forward. I managed to stop my momentum by putting both hands on the ground, but I did pay a toll. My breath left me and my chin took a more than slight tap.

I pushed myself up and crawled forward finding my balance. Before I had a chance to stand, Tyne had lifted me up.

"Oh, my chin hurts," I complained. I rubbed it, while everyone stared.

"How did you happen to land on the floor?" asked my mother. And that was a tough question to know how to answer because I thought I'd been pushed. "I'm not sure," I said. "Maybe I lost my balance." I gave Mom a look, and she nodded—she'd received my message.

"We'll talk later, Mile" she replied. I heard a few snickers. I understood the current thoughts regarding my clumsiness.

"Briny and I have protective gear, Major Craig. Why don't the rest of you retreat, and we'll open the front of the artifact. The most we'll face is some gases, so I'll call you when we're finished."

I thought Cam a little delusional thinking there would only be gas to face—there could be bombs or some such which would be triggered when the door opened—but no one asked for my opinion.

Cam and Briny began to suit up, while the rest of us retreated to the surface.

And I was glad to do so; my claustrophobia needed a rest. Of course, travel through the passageways was the worst for me—the cavern I'd handled with ease. With its high ceiling, my mind decided the roof wouldn't collapse.

We all plunked down on the ground when we reached the surface. Squid sat beside me. "Mile, are you okay? You seem a little pale."

"No problem. I just haven't had enough fluid today. I really need to watch my intake—I get dehydrated so easily and then feel woozy." I hoped my explanation would ease his concern. Actually, I wanted him to stop watching me, and pay attention to someone else. I had no desire for my claustrophobia to become common knowledge because it might affect my standing with the ESF. I certainly didn't want that to happen—I loved exploring alien worlds.

However, if Squid was going to pry, then so was I.

"Why did you join the ESF?" If I could warm him up, I had other questions burning a hole in my brain.

"My parents are members of EEF." After glancing at my face, he said, "EEF is Earth Explorations Force. They scope things out before the ESF is sent in to analyze what they've found. And since I have more of a scientific bent, I decided to join ESF."

I knew about the EEF, but his revelation regarding his family interested me. We all liked to follow in our parents' footsteps—to some extent.

Now for the million dollar question. "Squid, what's your real name, and why are you called Squid?"

"Ah, I wondered when you'd get around to being nosy about my name. It took you long enough."

His grin irritated me, so I glared at him.

"Okay, okay. My real name is Skerious Donald Acorne."

"Well, your names are certainly a mouthful, but I'm not seeing any reference to Squid. Care to enlighten me?"

Squid laughed. "I love fishing, and I love to eat squid, so the nickname just happened." He studied me after I didn't respond. "Can you really see being called Skerious would work with all the crazy people around us?"

I giggled. "You're right. Squid is much more appropriate."

Tyne came over and sat beside Squid and me. I tried to think of a topic to discuss that would include all three of us, but before we had a chance to converse, Cam and Briny returned carrying two bags each.

I jumped up. "What do you have?"

Cam ignored me and spoke to Major Craig. "My scanner detected no gases of any kind after we opened the shrine door. So we took off our helmets. Briny scrunched down and pulled out everything she could find."

They put down their bags and started emptying the contents. A mound of square tiles appeared.

"What do we have here?" asked Major Craig.

"A puzzle," announced Cam. "Our gamers will agree, I imagine, after they get a good look."

We all surged forward. "Stop," said Major Craig. "Cam, did you take pictures, or samples?"

"Not yet. Well, actually, we took a scan of the inside before Briny pulled everything out, but my main pictures and samples will be done after we return to the lab."

Sylone glanced at the rest of us. "Okay, let's return to the ship, and have a rest break. Well, except for Cam and Briny, of course. Then we'll meet at dinner time and study these discoveries."

No one argued, and we settled in the rover for our return trip.

****

Dinner was a lively affair. The whole staff, ship crew and all, had gathered—a rare occurrence. Normally, at least some of the ship staff wandered about doing security and whatever else they did. *Why is today a special day?*

Major Craig stood up. "I have an announcement. Although he tried to hide today's importance, Major White has been outed. Today's his birthday." The room cheered. "Now, he won't let me tell you the actual number, but let's just say it's a multiple of ten."

Hoots added to the cheers, and then Briny exited the kitchen alcove with a cake.

Slightly embarrassed, John passed around cake after we sang *Happy Birthday*.

"Happy Birthday, Major White." I smiled at him, after grabbing my piece of cake. "Now, can we get to the really important things?"

Laughter erupted. "Cam, tell us about the tiles," I demanded.

"You're going to like this, Mile. Actually, all our puzzlers will. I think we found another nonogram." Cam hesitated. "Well, maybe. A few of the pieces look like the outside edges of one."

I couldn't believe his words. Something strange was going on—we start solving nonograms and then they suddenly appear everywhere?

Squid said, "Let's make a big table and attempt the puzzle."

After looking at the surfaces of the pieces, we all agreed with Squid's conclusion of a nonogram.

We moved the tiles around like a three pot puzzle—try and find the pea under one of the containers. However, we weren't looking for a pea; we looked for a puzzle to solve.

Thankfully, we weren't under the control of a con artist. But were we? My mind considered the implications of my question.

Eventually, the edges of the puzzle became clear, and then the middle.

"This's definitely a nonogram," said Cam. "I wager a…. Well, I wager something as a prize for the first person to solve it." He took a picture and sent it to everyone.

The break room became eerily quiet. Although the thoughts piling up in the break room were almost verbal, I tried to ignore everyone. This particular puzzle had attracted my attention more than the others we'd worked on.

"Numbers," said Tyne.

Numbers? Numbers? After taking a second look at my scribbles, I decided Tyne was probably correct. "Yes, I think they are. Anyone else?"

"No collusion," said Mist.

I decided to ignore her. Knowing Mist, she might be mad at me, for some unknown reason. Unknown to me, anyway.

"First line," said Tyne, and sent everyone a text.

His description of *first line* was a little off. I think he meant first line of a readable text.

Cam replied, "Yes, I agree those are numbers. Okay, everyone, figure out the rest. I have a guess about where this is going, but I don't want to skew your perceptions."

We settled down to puzzle out the rest. After looking at Tyne's message, no one argued with his interpretation, and took it as a basis for their calculations.

"You guys are brilliant! We now have a set of coordinates," Cam said, after Tyne sent him his interpretation. "At far as I can tell."

Major White and Cam whispered and then retreated to the bridge—and a conversation with the ship's computer, I suspected.

The rest of us waited in the break room, somewhat impatiently.

After only a short time, John and Cam returned. "These're definitely the coordinates for another location on this planet. We're being pointed somewhere once again," Cam added.

Before Major Craig had a chance to respond, I asked, "Isn't this a little convenient? Everywhere we go, we're pointed to another location. When will this end?" My patience had started to run out.

"Actually," said Major White, "we believe we're part of two triangles. These coordinates point to a new location on this planet. Other coordinates have pointed to a new planet, as you may remember." John smiled, and I remembered our trip from Needles to Agora was based on a puzzle.

"Of course, I'm making quite a leap here, assuming we have three locations on Agora to explore, and another planet to explore. Only time will tell."

The whole group in the break room took John's statements under consideration. Still too convenient, I thought, but I kept my mouth shut.

Then everyone turned to look at Major Craig. Decision time.

"Adventure is our motto. Right?" she said. Silence was golden, in this case. She smiled, and said, "Tomorrow, we'll go to these new coordinates on Agora. Tonight, I send a message to Earth." She left the break room to return to her duties.

Such a comic. She'd made everyone laugh, diffused the tension that had developed over John's announcement regarding triangles, and told us what tomorrow would bring. My mother excelled in her position as leader.

I looked at my com to try and decide what to puzzle next. However, Tyne interrupted my thoughts.

"Dance?" he asked.

A Keeki dance? My heart soared. "Lovely," I said. "How shall I dress?"

Tyne hadn't a clue what I'd asked. "Now."

"Yes, yes. Let's go, but let me stash my stuff away."

Tyne followed me as I returned to my stateroom. Actually, he followed me inside. He closed my door, and approached me. His hand reached up to my face and began to stroke it.

"Tyne, what're you doing?"

"Pleasure," he responded.

"Does touching my skin please you?" I asked. My emotions whirled.

"*softness delight,*
exciting,
pleasure all mine?"

His words offered no confusion. "No, the pleasure is not just yours." I reached up and touched his face. In addition to the blue scales on the portions of his arms usually exposed, he had silky scales on his face. A whiff of lemon escaped after my gentle touch.

We continued to stroke cheeks, and then I said, "Let me touch your ear."

Moisture gathered in Tyne's eyes as I stroked.

"Okay?" I asked, after my brain re-engaged.

"*comforting feelings,*
happiness,
much, much pleasure."

He reached out and touched my ears with both of his hands.

Although I'd never thought of ears as particularly erogenous, I turned out to be wrong, wrong, wrong.

I desperately wanted to continue our exploration, but reality intruded. “Perhaps it’s time to try out the dance you wanted me to join.”

He grabbed my hand. “Now.”

“Now is good,” I said, although I did notice his reluctance to leave my room.

We journeyed outside, and talked to the guard as we passed through the doorway. Tyne grabbed my hand and pulled me towards the rear of *Skyfall*. As we rounded the tail, I discovered a grassy flat area. Most of the ship’s Keeki contingent had gathered there, and they obviously waited for the two of us.

Tyne grabbed my hand, and the other Keeki paired up.

One of the Keeki started singing—apparently the cue for the dancing to begin.

Thankfully, their dancing reminded me of a waltz—slow and steady and rhythmic. I also understood why our translator interpreted their speaking in a two word / one word / three words structure—their singing consisted of the same form. Quite a revelation, actually. Perhaps I needed to mention this to my mother.

I had a hard time trying to understand what the singer tried to express, so I just went with the flow and allowed Tyne to guide my dancing.

Eventually, the singing died down, and so did the dancing.

Tyne and I watched the Keeki disappear—back to *Skyfall*, I suspected.

He caught my eye,

“*large rock,*

sitting,

exploring species desires.”

I’d actually noticed the rock while we’d danced, so we wandered over.

Tyne grabbed my hand and pressed it on his cheek—I was happy to comply. Eventually, I taught my favorite Keeki how to kiss. And that’s how we spent the rest of our evening.

Chapter Fifteen

water unnerving
upsetting
sailing together appropriate

The next morning dawned sunny and clear. As I thought about the situation, I didn't remember experiencing any rain during our sojourn on Agora. I reminded myself to talk to Major White about weather patterns, or at least quiz him on what he'd found out so far.

By spaceship, we had a short trip to our new landing spot. *Skyfall* sat down between the shore and a forest. This shoreline had lots of sand and a shiny, white glow. The ocean's color reminded me of a green-blue—much like other areas we'd seen. The forest, on the other hand, had a distinct red hue. Was this normal? A fall color? Actually, what season were we experiencing? I had many questions to ask our resident experts.

"Anyone object if I declare today a rest day?" asked Major Craig.

Laughter bounced around our gathering on the shore.

"I didn't think so. I know our last try was not that restful, so another is needed. I know I need a break. Go jump in the ocean, or take long walks. Get lots of exercise. If you do find something interesting take pictures and notes. Please do not go off alone; groups are safer. Have a great day!" Mom grinned and went back into the ship.

Now what was I going to do? I studied the area and noticed a decent breeze from the ocean. I also saw a nearby sparkling island.

Turning around I spied Major White, and galloped off in his direction.

"Major White? I have a question," I said.

"Mile, I think you can call me John, by now—at least, in an informal situation. What's up?"

I gave him a smile. "I don't suppose you happen to have any sailboats on our ship, do you? Even small ones?"

"Why?" Major White focused his attention on me.

"Ah, I'd like to go sailing. There's a pretty good breeze, and an island close by, so a perfect opportunity for an adventure. Anything available?"

"Actually, I do have a solution. Come with me."

My mood improved immensely as we traipsed back into the ship, and down into one of the cargo holds. I knew the holds existed, but I had no idea what they contained.

John pulled a large box out from a shelf, and plopped it on the floor.

"I have what you need," he said. "This is an inflatable boat we always carry. And…" He turned away and grabbed another box from the same shelf. "And your necessary items, mast, rudder, and sail, to complete your sailboat."

"Seriously?" I couldn't believe my eyes.

"Yes, Mile." A smile graced his face. "This boat is self-inflating, and I'm sure you'll be able to figure out how to put the mast and such together to have a nice sail."

"You're the best, Major, ah John. I'll bring it back in one piece, I promise." I grinned from ear to ear—today was going to be a good day. I almost gave him a hug, but thought better of it.

We both grabbed a box and proceeded outside to the shoreline. We dumped the objects on the ground, and then John disappeared. I took a moment, but I eventually figured out how to inflate the sailboat. Not a bad size—big enough for two or three, at least.

"What do we have here?" asked Squid, startling me.

"A sailboat. Today is my day for being on the water. I got these from Major White. Apparently, there are wonders to be found in the holds of *Skyfall*."

"I like sailing. May I join you?" asked Squid.

"Sure. Help me put the parts together." I decided I had no reason to discourage him. He wasn't my first choice as a companion, but I actually liked Squid.

Squid and I worked for a while inflating the rest of the parts, and then Tyne wandered our way. "What?" he asked.

"Oh, this's a sailboat. The winds help it glide upon a water surface. I just love sailing." I wondered if he had any idea what my words meant.

I studied Tyne as he studied the sailboat. Did I see a little fear on his face? What the hell, I decided. "Do you want to join us, Tyne? Squid and I are going sailing."

His glance at Squid told me quite a lot. "Yes," Tyne replied. Jealousy ran rampant amongst the boys.

Today would add to my diplomatic experience, I decided. "Okay. Let's get this boat on the road. Okay, on the water." I laughed at my joke, even though no one else did.

"First, though, let's all pack for the day—food and fluid and such. And I need to talk to Major White before we leave," said Squid. We all ran back to *Skyfall*.

After we congregated on the beach, Squid and I pushed the sailboat out a little. Tyne stood frozen on the shore. "Squid, let's get Tyne on deck, I don't think he's the least bit comfortable with our adventure."

"No problem. Being a bird, sort of, the water probably freaks him out."

We eased Tyne onto one of the inflatable benches attached to the floor of our conveyance. Although the sailboat was small, it had plenty of room for a passenger and two crew.

"Okay?" I asked Tyne.

I received a nod—probably the most positive confirmation I'd receive for the next little while.

"Squid, prepare to steer. I'll give us a push." I jumped out and grabbed onto the back of the sailboat.

In no time, we started moving, and I climbed inside and sat beside Tyne.

"Okay?" I asked again. Then I thought about my question. Perhaps I shouldn't point out the possible negatives but just let him enjoy the view and whatever else he thought about.

Tyne glanced at me, and then said,

"*water unnerving,*

upsetting,

sailing together appropriate."

He wanted to be with me, and his feelings overrode his fears! My fondness for Tyne grew.

"Squid, how about steering us towards that island? I see sparkles in my future." We all laughed. My fondness for sparkly things wasn't a secret.

"Will do, Captain Mile. Landing in thirty minutes or so." Squid gave me a salute. "I see digging in sand in our future." Squid made adjustments and kept us aimed in the right direction.

I had to laugh. What a character! I turned to Tyne and tried to gauge his reactions. He didn't seem too upset, so the three of us continued to sail in a companionable silence. Then I said, "Will you help me look for sparkly things after we land?"

"Yes. Soon?" His hands gripped the edge of the bench.

No misunderstanding here—Tyne needed off the sailboat. "Squid?"

"We should land in less than five minutes. Make sure your lifejackets are tight—just in case we have a hard landing." Squid turned away to focus on his sailing.

"Tyne, are you okay? Can I do anything right now? We'll be landing soon."

"Fine." He didn't look at me, or the ocean, but kept his glance on the floor of the sailboat.

Well, Tyne didn't look fine to me, but I couldn't do anything for him, at the moment.

Shortly, we touched down on the island's shore. We helped Tyne out, and beached our sailboat.

We were all starving, so we dug into our packs and rummaged for food. The ocean, fresh air, and a beach to explore, put me in one of my happy places.

Soon, Squid and I realized Tyne had fallen asleep on his pack. He looked comfortable and unstressed, so we sneaked away and started looking for shiny stuff. We didn't go far, and I kept an eye on Tyne.

I stopped digging to take a good look at the ocean and our surroundings. "I really love these islands, Squid. They must be wonderful places to explore. I hope we get to stay a while, and not jump up and travel to another location too soon. I need a little stability."

A sigh escaped. Our day of rest was definitely needed. Then my curiosity got the better of me. "Squid, you told me your real name recently, and why your nickname is Squid, but I think you're hiding something. Is there another reason for Squid to stick to you?"

We both laughed at my combining the words Squid and sticking.

"Apparently, from the day I was born, I've always squirmed like a squid—at least according to my mother. Actually, she said I squirmed before I was born, too. And that translated into swimming. I love the water and water sports, and, and … all sorts of other stuff."

"So you feel comfortable being called Squid?"

"Sure. I've been called Squid more times than my real name."

"I guess Squid kind of rhymes with Skerious. Is Donald one of your father's names?"

"Yeah, how did you know?"

"Just a wild guess. Here's another guess—your mother reads fantasy and came up with Skerious from some book or other."

"She won't admit where she found the name, but I know it resonates with her. I suspect she made it up, and my father agreed." Squid took a long look at me. "Mile, your guesses are amazing. You need to meet my mother. I think you'd get along."

"Sure, sounds like a plan when we get back to Earth." I needed to change the subject, but before I had a chance, Tyne joined us.

"Feeling better?" I asked. His color had returned to Keeki normal.

"*body imbalance,*
restoring,
equilibrium with fluids."

Okay, I decided he felt better. "Will you be okay if we take another sail? The biggest island in this group is really close by. I have good feelings about what we might find."

No arguments from either Squid or Tyne, so we set off.

Chapter Sixteen

underwater life
taste
not to liking

Our day continued sunny and beautiful. The wind had started to pick up, and I enjoyed the breeze on my face. Glancing at Squid, he obviously embraced the extra air movement for his sailing. His enjoyment of being on the ocean was evident.

"Mile, I got a fishing rod and tackle from Major White. So after I drop you two on the island, I'm going to take the sailboat back out and go fishing."

"Aren't you the clever one? I wonder what else Major White has hidden in the holds?"

"I only got the idea of fishing after you scouted out a boat. However, your question is a good one. Maybe Major White will let us snoop around. After all, what we find might help us in our exploring."

"And that's probably a tactful way to suggest it to Major White." I laughed, and added, "And I know you like to rummage around as much as I do. So don't forget about me when you get permission."

We settled into a companionable silence until Tyne stood. "Perhaps you should sit down," I suggested.

"Seat," Tyne said, pointing to one closer to the bow.

I shrugged. The sailboat's movement might affect Tyne less up front, and that would help him acquire his sea legs.

He struggled to move a couple of yards, and then he tripped and fell overboard.

"Squid!" I yelled. "Man overboard. I mean Keeki!" I struggled to calm myself.

"I see him, and I'm turning right now." Squid competently executed his maneuver. Thankfully, Tyne had remained floating on the surface, so we pulled him aboard.

We checked the Keeki out, as best we could. Tyne appeared to be breathing easily, so I said, "Squid, make for the big island, as fast as you can."

He nodded and returned to his sailing. Thankfully, the island was close.

I pulled Tyne against me. He coughed a bit, but didn't appear to be in much distress. "Tyne, talk to me."

"*underwater life,*

taste,

not to liking."

His kaiku made me laugh; no ambiguousness there.

"Yeah, well I just might not take you sailing again. In the meantime, we'll soon be on shore, and you can rest."

And soon it was. Squid and I helped Tyne off the sailboat and found him a comfortable place to sit. Nearby, we found an expansive flat area. Tyne didn't appear to be in any distress, but I decided to call my mother anyway.

"Squid, please keep an eye on Tyne. I'm calling Major Craig."

He nodded and sat beside Tyne.

"Major Craig, we have a slight problem." I didn't want to alarm her.

"What happened, Mile?"

"Ah, Tyne fell off the sailboat, but Squid and I rescued him. We're all safely on shore now. Tyne doesn't to have any symptoms, but a medical examination might be in order."

"Where are you?" Her concern was evident to me.

"We're on the Big Island," I said. "Here are the coordinates." I knew we could be tracked, but I decided tact was in order. "Squid and I found a flat area perfect for *Skyfall* to land on."

"Okay. Let me gather everyone up, and then we'll be on our way. Keep Tyne warm."

Warm confused me, but I didn't argue.

Then Major White called and discussed the proposed landing spot.

Briny was the first out of *Skyfall* and ran over to Tyne. She talked to him for a bit, and then the two of them stood and walked toward the spaceship. Briny gave me a thumbs-up, so I knew Tyne would be okay.

The rest of our crew milled about and examined the nearby areas of the island. Then I heard, "Mile, I need to talk to you," said my mother. "Let's walk that way."

I didn't really grasp where she pointed, but I followed her.

"Mile, what happened today?" Concern filled her voice.

"Nothing much. Tyne's not much of a sailor, and when he decided to move forward on the sailboat, he fell off. Squid turned us around and we rescued him. Not that it was much of a rescue. He seems pretty okay to me, and Briny seems to agree."

"Yes. Just an unfortunate incident." Mom studied my face.

"Perhaps I shouldn't have taken him out. Descending from a bird-like species should have been a trigger." I second-guessed my actions.

"Why? Birds like water. Remember the bird baths we used to have?"

"Apparently, these aliens have issues with water. However, Tyne did agree to go along with Squid and me. You know, maybe he's the bravest of us all." My thoughts reminded me of Tyne going up the mountain with the humans. He really was brave—trying to overcome his Keeki inhibitions. "I don't know what else I could've decided," I said.

"Yes, you should've had a perfect day. Too bad it was spoiled. However, I do need to discuss the ramifications of Tyne's dumping."

Alarmed, I said, "What do you mean?"

"Aran, the leader of the Keeki, came to me and had words. Many words—quite unlike what I'd expect from someone of their race. He wanted me to tell you to stay away from Tyne."

"Aran, huh. You know, I think he pushed me a second time when we were down in the caves."

"Agreed. Your actions there surprised me. I've never seen you that clumsy before. However, I should abide by the wishes of the Keeki leader."

"But, Mom, Tyne and I are friends." I had an urge to shed a few tears.

"Yes. I know you and Tyne have much in common." She smiled. "Let's just say, what I don't see, I don't know about."

Mom gave me a hug. "In the meantime, I'm going to talk to Earth. The way Aran's going, I suspect he'll want to segregate the Keeki from humans—and that's not the point of this expedition."

She rubbed her forehead. "Anyway, go clean up. It's time for dinner, and I'm sure the fresh air has made everyone hungry."

We strode back to the ship. I certainly needed a cleanup. Wandering in and out of the water all day had deposited sand and sweat all over my body. I hoped a long relaxing shower would relieve my anxiety regarding a number of issues.

I sat with Squid, Cam, and Briny at dinner, and studied the break room. Mist sat with Tyne, and I realized the segregation had begun. I really hoped no one would blame me—no one other than Aran.

"What's going on, Mile?" asked Squid. "Why isn't Tyne sitting with us? He almost always does. Is he upset about falling in the ocean?"

"Aran doesn't want me talking to Tyne. Apparently, I threw him in the water, or something like that."

"That's ridiculous. Tyne was uncomfortable sailing, and made a mistake, or misstep, I guess you could call it," said Squid.

"I know. But, in the meantime, he's supposed to stay away from me. However, I'm sure M…Major Craig will get the situation settled in record time."

"Want to work on some puzzles after dinner?" asked Squid.

Puzzles, yeah. "Sounds like a good idea. However, I want to take a walk first. I spent a lot of time sitting on that sailboat today, and I need to stretch my legs."

"I'll join you," said Squid.

Not sure I wanted company, nonetheless I didn't respond in a negative way. I had a lot to think about, and none of the topics involved Squid.

"Let's check out the lake first," I said. During our discussion regarding the landing spot, Major White had pointed out his discoveries on the big island, and his information had included a lake. Squid and I walked toward the body of water, in a companionable silence.

Spotting the Keeki doing their evening dance, I pointed Squid in a roundabout direction. Of interest to me, I didn't notice Aran amongst the group.

It didn't take long to arrive at the water feature. "Let's walk part of the way around the lake. I want to see if there are any beaches filled with sparkly things."

"A little delusional, Mile, but you may be correct," commented Squid, giving me a smile.

We walked quite a distance before we spotted a likely candidate. Most of the shoreline had proved to be rocks and drop offs, but we eventually came upon a small beach.

I dumped my backpack and rummaged about until I found my trowel and gloves. Digging in the sand gave me much pleasure. So Squid and I messed up the beach for half an hour. We found a diverse group of small stones during our endeavor.

"Okay, I think we've collected enough for us and Cam. I know he'd want some for analysis," I said. "How about we keep walking, and get a bit more exercise?"

Hearing no argument from Squid, we continued around the lake, and then came to a hole in the ground.

"What's this, Squid?" An open area—really a depression in the ground—surprised us.

"I don't know, but I do see stairs disappearing downwards. Do you?"

The round opening was wide, so a lot of light trickled down. Where did this circular stairway go?

Squid asked, "How many levels do you think there are?" We both peered into the opening, but counting proved difficult from the top.

"There's only one way we're going to find out." Another adventure for my day.

We trundled down and stopped at the first level. The circular path was wide enough that anyone—at least human or Keeki—could sit on its edge dangling their feet, and there would be ample room for others to pass behind.

Eventually the two of us reached the bottom of the stairway. Squid and I sat on the lowest level and studied the open center. I glanced up to gauge our downward travel distance. We'd come a lot farther than I'd imagined.

Before Squid and I had a chance to discuss our surroundings, we heard a shout. We waved Cam and Briny down to join us.

A few moments later, the excited duo sat beside us.

"You know, guys, this is like an amphitheater for plays. Or maybe the inhabitants used the stairs and roundabouts as an exercise regime." Everyone laughed at my second suggestion.

"You're probably right about the plays, Mile. Although this area could also be used to hold meetings, auctions, performances, lots of things," said Cam. "We have no idea what cultural performances an alien nation could need." Cam paused, and then said, "This area, and the stairs could be used for some ritual beyond our understanding."

Cam was correct. We needed to keep an open mind, as difficult as it could be.

And then slave auction came to mind. With no idea why, I decided to keep my thought to myself.

Cam broke into my reverie. "Look around. I see markings on the walls of each level."

I jumped down, and glanced at the wall under where my seat. "Here, too," I pointed. Why hadn't I seen any of them on our way down?

"I'm going to take a million pictures. When we get back and explain what we found to Major Craig, I'm sure she'll want everyone to gather here tomorrow and analyze this structure and its markings."

"Good idea, Cam. The rest of us can take pictures, too. Amongst all of us, the big picture should emerge." I pulled out my camera.

After finishing my picture taking, I turned around and found Tyne sitting on the lowest ledge. How long had he been there?

"Agora to Mile, Agora to Mile," said Cam.

After a couple of repetitions, I finally heard Cam. "What?" Why did he bother me?

"The rest of us are going back to the ship. Coming?" asked Cam.

"Ah, I think I'll stay here for a while. I want to drink in the atmosphere."

Cam coughed, or choked, or made a noise I didn't want to think about. "Sure. Just don't stay too long, or Major Craig will send us back to find you. And, ah, it might be a good idea to come back alone."

Apparently, I wasn't fooling anyone, except myself.

Cam, Briny, and Squid climbed up and out, and then I went over to Tyne and sat beside him.

"Tyne, are you feeling all right? After your dump in the ocean, I mean?"

"*missing you,*
unhappy,

not appreciate Aran."

His words were easy to understand. "I know. Major Craig doesn't think much of his demand, either. After all, ours is a combined expedition. And what we do in our off time is none of his business."

He stared at me.

"Ah, Major Craig is going to talk to Earth about the situation. Hopefully, it'll get resolved very soon."

He reached out and stroked my cheek, so I reciprocated.

I sighed. "I think we'd better get back to base. Otherwise, they might start sending out search parties."

Tyne grabbed my right hand.

"*heart soul,*

sadness,

spend time together."

I placed my left hand on his. "I'm also upset about Aran's decision. I really want to spend a great deal of time with you. We're going to have to find ways, make them. However, right now, we need to get back."

I leaned over to give him a quick kiss, but he pulled me up and proceeded to kiss me thoroughly.

Eventually, I said, "I need to go back. Follow me, in a moment."

Tyne released me, reluctantly, and I started up the stairway. Wrenching my emotions back into some kind of control, I progressed up the amphitheater stairway.

Glancing back, I caught Tyne's smile. I decided to ignore Aran's order.

Chapter Seventeen

similar logic
mindfulness
Keeki and humans

Back at the ship, I wandered into the break room.

"Mile, it's about time you showed up. I've been explaining to Major Craig and everyone what you and Squid just discovered. I've started sending out the pictures I took of the specific wall markings. I know you took panoramic pictures, why don't you send those. Then whoever hasn't seen what we saw can put it all together in their minds," ordered Cam, before I had a chance to utter a word.

I dumped my pack on a chair and rummaged for my com. After sending everyone my pictures, I looked at Cam's.

"What do you think these markings are?" I asked him. "Is this one long stream, maybe starting from the top layer and winding around the levels?"

He shook his head. "I don't think so. What's popped into my mind is nonograms."

Cam's comment percolated amongst the group in the break room.

"I think we've found a wondrous structure. Artificial, if you will. And I think we need to study all the pictures to see if any pattern is evident," I said. "Maybe these markings are just artistic endeavors."

The break room became as quiet as a church. Then Cam said, "They're nonograms; I'm sure of it. Look here and here." He projected a couple of my pictures on the one blank wall of the break room.

Then he projected a couple of colored lines. "If you put these together, you get a nonogram. I bet the whole amphitheater markings indicate a story. Perhaps something performed there."

"Sure do look like nonograms, more or less. We need to figure out how the pieces go together—kind of like a jigsaw puzzle nonogram."

A lot of groans sounded—the solution would not be easy, even if Cam's guess was correct. "Does anyone think this's a little too convenient?"

"What do you mean, Mile?" asked Cam.

"Well, we've been working on nonograms and jigsaw puzzles for the last weeks, and now we're starting to run into them everywhere we go. I find it hard to believe that another culture, or alien race I guess, would have exactly the same kind of games or puzzles as we do."

"*similar logic,*
mindfulness,
Keeki and humans," said Tyne. He'd joined us a few moments after I'd returned to the ship.

"Actually, you're right. Our nonograms were slightly different than yours, but we made the concept fit both." I decided to leave the subject alone for now, but I was still convinced another force was at work affecting our lives.

Mom gave me a speculative glance—she obviously understood my thoughts. I suspected her impressions coincided with mine.

"Okay, let's try and decipher this mess. Cam, how do you think we should start?" I asked.

Squid had the brilliant idea of printing off Cam's pictures, and cutting them up into pieces, while Briny suggested labelling each piece with some kind of reference so we knew where they fitted inside the amphitheater. We put a couple of tables together and, before long, the nonograms became obvious.

Cam said, "Okay, looks like we have six nonograms to solve. Everyone in?"

No objections were voiced. "I'll divvy them out and we can have a contest to see who finishes theirs first. They don't look very hard, and the information provided doesn't seem to have many gaps. Grab some food and drink, and we'll have a race."

Having a race seemed a bit counterproductive, but I didn't argue. A portion of my coworkers loved competitions.

After a relatively short time, Cam announced, "Squid is the winner, but you were all pretty fast. Let's put our solutions in the middle of the table, so we can study them."

After a moment, I said, "These are all numbers. What do they mean?"

"Probably coordinates, I'm guessing," said Cam.

"How do we figure out the order?" A previous nonogram had pointed us in a new direction, and I was curious if this one would do the same.

"Good question," said Squid.

The break room was quiet while brains engaged to consider my question.

"Let's try putting them in order from the top of the amphitheater. At least, it's a start," suggested Cam.

Briny's idea of marking their locations proved invaluable as we worked on this strange jigsaw puzzle.

"Hmm," said Cam, after we'd finished. "I'm going to take a picture of our solution, and then let's put it together again from the bottom up."

Two different sets of numbers resulted.

"Cam, how can we tell which is right? Should we try and put the nonograms together in another combination? Maybe alternating?" I asked. I struggled with the myriad possibilities.

"I'll take our two current possibilities to Major White and we'll put them through the nav computer."

"Do these numbers relate to this planet or another location out in space somewhere?" I asked.

Cam laughed. "Maybe another galaxy? Let's see what the computations give us. I'll be back shortly."

He left the room. The rest of us needed to pass the time while we anxiously awaited the results, so I asked, "How about a jigsaw puzzle? I need something a little brainless, right now. Anyone have a puzzle we can work on?"

Mist waved and left the room. What did her actions mean? I sent a glance toward Tyne.

"*Keeki puzzle,*
retrieving,
enjoyment for all."

I think I understood his words, so I decided to wait a few moments before finding something else to do.

Mist soon returned carrying a box. She dumped the contents on our table. Puzzle pieces galore flooded the surface.

"Do we have a picture of the final product?" I asked, picking up one of the pieces.

"No." Mist seemed amused by my question.

Okay, that would make her puzzle a bit of a challenge—especially since the pieces of a Keeki jigsaw were more angular than I was used to.

I loved the gorgeous colors of her pieces, but I had no idea about the puzzle's subject. However, Tyne jumped in and started putting pieces together in record time. I watched his movements hoping to find an idea of the focus of Mist's puzzle.

While I did, I wondered, *Will Aran be upset with Tyne for frequenting the same table as I do?*

Such a weird, and wonderful, world I occupied. I thought back to my recent first contact course, and I decided the writers had never been in a first contact situation.

Possibly a little naïve, but I'd certainly be willing to give suggestions for improvement of the material.

The puzzle was still unfinished when Cam and Majors White and Craig showed up.

"Lovely picture," commented Major Craig. "Somewhere on Keeki?"

Mist nodded. Her action reminded me I wanted to talk to Mom about her knowledge of Keeki culture.

"From the expectant glances I'm receiving, I have a lot of curious expedition members. Let me relieve the tension. The coordinates you've deciphered point to a fairly close planet."

She waited for the murmurs to subside. "We're going on another trip."

Moans and groans floated around the room.

"I'm not too happy myself. We've barely scratched the surface of this planet, and I mean barely. However, something is going on and we're going to figure it out. I'll be sending a message to Earth this evening outlining our plans. I'm also going to say to them, this is *it*! No more wandering about the galaxy. We need to explore in depth the planets we've already discovered."

Mom took a deep breath. "We'll see how they respond to my ultimatum. In the meantime, tomorrow will be the start of another adventure."

Conversations murmured throughout the break room.

"Regardless of Earth's response, we're leaving tomorrow. Early, as usual." Mom grinned. "Just one final comment." She paused for a moment, and then said, "I'm starting to agree with Mile's conclusion—we're being manipulated. I have no idea by whom, but we're going to find out."

Mom's sobering statement about agreeing with me gave me pause for thought—I really hoped we weren't being pushed around.

Chapter Eighteen

unknown future
Wyre
means complete enlightenment

Our journey to our next destination would take about a day and half. On the first day of our trip I found most of the expedition cranky, and the situation lasted all day.

"We haven't had any decent amount of time for exploration on any of the planets. And now we're going to another one?" Squid whined. "This is so not what I expected on my first off-planet expedition."

"When we return, we'll have stories to tell," I said. "Our classmates will be envious."

We had a final year of classes before we graduated. When we returned from this expedition, all our classmates would've returned from theirs. One-upmanship would last for a few weeks.

On the other hand, we had no idea now when our expedition would end.

Squid didn't indicate any agreement, and continued to sulk. Mist and Tyne sat at a nearby table, and that's all they were doing—sitting. Not talking, not working on any projects, as far as I could tell. Was Aran's edict having an effect?

However, the long evening ahead of us still needed to be endured, so we needed something to occupy our time. "How about a game night? Or even a tournament?"

"Sounds like a plan," said Squid, glancing at the other tables.

I got his message and stood. "Everyone, it's time for another of our infamous game nights. Let's figure out a format, and a prize, of course."

Eventually, we agreed upon a tournament involving three board games. Each participant would receive points based upon their final standing in each game, and the player with the most points would be awarded a prize. After much discussion, the three games agreed upon would be *Uno, Ticket to Ride,* and a Keeki game called *Wampa*—a game never before played.

While playing *Wampa*, a game of finding treasures in an underground cavern, with Tyne and Cam, I asked, "What do you think we should call this new planet? We need to think up something interesting before Earth comes up with a name, or number."

"Do we know anything about this planet?" asked Cam.

"If anyone did, wouldn't it be our chief scientist?" I asked, giving Cam a smirk.

"You'd think so—so I could prepare the lab—but I know nothing. This is the weirdest expedition I've ever been on."

After two decades, Cam had experienced quite a few, I remembered.

Then Tyne said,

"*unknown future,*

Wyre,

means complete enlightenment."

"I like your idea of W*yre*," said Cam. "We have no clue about what's going to happen, and we really want to be enlightened. I'll take your suggestion up with Major Craig tomorrow."

At the conclusion of our game night, Mist claimed champion status.

"Now, what are we going to do about a prize?" I asked.

"I've been thinking about that topic," said Cam. "How about I use the science lab's 3D printer to print a medallion, and then we can add a ribbon. We can make up something pretty cool."

A positive consensus was reached, with offers of design help from a couple of participants.

"Sounds like a plan. And let's make up first, second, and third medallions. The points tonight were very close, so we should acknowledge more players," I suggested.

The break room's hum increased—my plan had worked.

"I don't know about anyone else, but this competition has tired me out. Bed time for me," I said. "When you have nothing to do, think up plans for our next competition. I need to earn medallions." Laughter followed my comments. Everyone began picking up the games and then leaving, so they were on the same page. We needed a good rest before tomorrow's arrival at a new planet.

I packed up my *Ticket To Ride* as the room gradually emptied. Soon Tyne and I were the only ones remaining.

"*painting creating,*
enjoyment,
present for you."

Tyne took a box out of a pocket and handed it to me.

My hands held the box he'd worked on at our last painting session. Striking designs and hues of blue and green covered the small box.

"Tyne, this's gorgeous. Is this for me?"

"Affirmation."

I glanced around the break room, and recognized we were the only remaining crew, so I took a leap.

"Tyne, I'm going back to my cabin. Would you like to join me?"

Apparently the answer was *yes*, as he grabbed my hand.

****

The next morning I found Major White alone at a table in the break room. I summoned up my courage and asked if I could join him on the bridge sometime. A mystery to me—I wanted to understand more of how the ship ran.

"Walk with me," he said, picking up his dishes and depositing them in the dishwasher.

Was I in trouble? We exited the break room and found some privacy.

"Why don't you join me around eleven? We'll be in orbit, and you can get a look at the planet and the bridge then." A small smile graced his face.

"Won't we be landing?" I didn't want to interfere with bridge operations.

"Eventually, but procedures indicate we traverse once around the planet before we make any decisions. You can sit in a back corner, watch the operations, and study the view screen."

"Wonderful. I'll be there." I wanted to dance around the corridor.

"Don't tell anyone. I don't need the whole expedition on the bridge."

Even better than I'd imagined, I said, "I owe you one."

John smiled and walked away.

A little presumptuous on my part, I realized a little belatedly. What value would I have to the ship's captain? Why should he allow me on the bridge? A teaching experience, I decided to ease my anxiety.

As I anxiously awaited the appointed time, my productivity declined. After arriving at the bridge, I stepped inside but, unsure of where I should go, I went no further.

"Come in, Cadet," said Major White. "We're pretty busy right now, so it's best if you just plunk yourself down in our visitor's chair." He pointed to the corner.

I nodded my thanks, and slipped into the seat.

The bridge wasn't particularly large but then neither was our ship. I saw three crew stations. I assumed Major White knew all procedures and could take over any one of them, as needed. He sat at one of the modules but, perhaps, that one was reserved for himself, the captain.

I listened to the minimal bridge chatter for a while, but I soon turned my attention to the large view screen.

We definitely orbited a planet. As we circled the planet, I watched the view screen and many continents came into view. The frozen poles interested me.

"Cadet Carter, do you have any questions?" asked Major White. His question startled me. I'd been engrossed in the view screen.

"Why is there so little water? I mean, I see lots of continents, and the poles, but very little in the way of bodies of water like oceans."

"Intriguing question, and very astute of you to notice. I have no answer. Of course, we really shouldn't think of Earth as anything like normal. Perhaps our home is unusual."

We both laughed. "Being explorers gives us access to many oddities," he added.

"And being part of ESF is our way to this access," I said. "I do appreciate you allowing me on the bridge."

"No problem. I must get back to work, however." He smiled and returned to his station.

After scanning the view screen for another hour, I slipped off the bridge, after waving a goodbye to Major White.

I found my mother in the break room, alone at a table. I grabbed lunch and asked to join her.

"Of course, Cadet." She pointed at the chair across from her.

"Major White allowed me on the bridge today. The views were spectacular. I should've asked for access when we were arriving at

Needles and Agora. It's given me a better perspective, and should help my understanding when we're on the ground."

"Indeed. I watched our approach from my cabin. An interesting planet, wouldn't you say?"

"Yes, yes. I especially liked the frozen areas. Can we land and do some skiing?" One of the sports I loved.

"That's not our first stop."

Seeing the disappointment on my face, Mom added, "This planet's space beacon points to a different area, so that's where we're going first. I'm sure we'll find time to visit one of the poles or, probably the way our expedition is going, be pointed there."

"This has been a strange expedition—not that I'm any expert, of course."

"I have to agree with you, and I have some expertise." Mom laughed. "And you should remember some of the *normal* ones I dragged you on."

We thought about our words for a couple of minutes. "I have to admit, though, it's been great in so many ways," I commented.

"Like what?" Mom cocked her head.

"Oh, seeing new worlds, meeting new aliens, exploring—all the things I like, and want, to do."

"Did meeting new aliens top your list?"

"Perhaps. Probably." I started to babble.

"We need to discuss your life pretty soon," said my mother, in a quiet voice. "But now, and here, is not the time or place."

I knew what she'd tried to express. "Yes, I have a few topics." More than a few to be honest with myself.

A mother-daughter bonding moment; we needed more of them.

Squid plopped into the chair beside me. "Major Craig, when are we landing? I thought it was supposed to be midday?"

"Major White wants to do another run around the planet. He found some anomalies, so he's going to take a pass over other areas. We'll land around dinner time."

"Okay, sounds logical. Mile, want to take another look at some puzzles we haven't solved? I have some ideas about a different approach."

"Yes, of course. I've finished eating, so let's grab another table." We moved away after saying goodbye to Major Craig.

Until I heard Major White's announcement regarding our landing, I hadn't realized how quickly the afternoon had flown. Squid's ideas about the puzzles had made my brain hurt but had certainly engaged me.

We all rushed to the viewing screen. Watching our landings had become one of my addictions. Of course, I hadn't expected quite this many. My new perspective, resulting from being on the bridge, had educated me about this new planet in quite a unique way.

Major Craig said, "Tomorrow will be a big day for exploration. I'll let you know in the morning what and where we'll focus. Now, have some dinner and then go exploring. Cam has confirmed breathability. Please do not venture far. Keep *Skyfall* in your sights."

I gobbled down dinner and then went back to my room and grabbed my backpack. I added water and a snack from the galley.

Outside, I did a random spin and apparently I needed to head south. I had no idea if my direction was actually south, but my pirouette determined my path.

I wandered along, in peace with myself. With little quiet time in recent memory, I needed a break.

Following the shoreline of the strange shaped continent we'd landed on, I studied the sand at my feet. A pretty dirty looking area stretched before me. Not a sparkle to be seen. So I changed my route to veer away from the ocean.

I traipsed along my new path, humming away. I rarely sang or hummed since I couldn't keep a tune. I had the annoying skill of being able to tell when I was off key. However, song did occasionally break out when I was happy and relaxed.

In the distance, an apparent meadow appeared, so I picked up my pace. The land within my view was relatively flat and arid.

Startled by movement to my right, I recognized the Keeki, out for their evening dancing. They synchronized a few hundred feet away—far enough to afford privacy.

Why did I desire privacy? I wanted to dig in the dirt, by myself. The activity would add to my calmness—much like gardening. I took a glance towards the Keeki, but I recognized their concentration, so I pulled out my trowel and started digging.

Since there was little surface to scoop away, I soon began my serious dig. I scraped for thirty minutes, and then began to find objects. I piled them on a sheet pulled from my backpack. After retrieving a number of objects I decided to quit digging. I sat back and studied my findings.

"Fossils!" I shrieked. As I dug, I hadn't really looked at what I'd pulled out of the soil—my mind had settled into a meditative state.

The Keeki turned my way and stopped dancing. Tyne and Mist ran over to my location.

"Guys, these are fossils." I pointed to my sheet. "This whole area is a fossil bed. We need to stop defiling it and mount a proper excavation. I'm calling Major Craig. Stop your dancing."

Tyne turned to Mist, and they returned to the other Keeki.

I called Major Craig. "I've found a fossil site. The Keeki were dancing on it, but they've stopped. We need to protect the site. Put barriers around it, or something."

"Mile, take a breath. Let me round up the rest of the troops and we'll be there shortly."

Little time passed before the troops gathered. With the help of the Keeki, we marked the most likely perimeter.

"It's getting dark, so let's return to the ship," said Major Craig. "We can discuss this discovery in the break room."

Chapter Nineteen

physical connection
missing
dearth of touch

The next morning, excitement permeated the conversations about the fossil bed I'd discovered. After breakfast, we grabbed our packs and took a brisk walk.

"Your tasks for today will be to excavate a portion of the outside edge," said Major Craig. "I have made assignments. The information should now be on your coms."

I glanced at my mother after I read my com. She nodded and then turned away. For some reason, Tyne and I comprised a team today. Tyne was as surprised as I was by our pairing.

We walked to our designated spot, far away from the other teams.

"*physical connection,*
missing,
dearth of touch."

I also missed Tyne's touch. I didn't respond verbally, but I thought about finding alone time later.

At lunch time, the excavating teams gathered for a break, and to compare findings.

Our reports ranged all over. One group found mounds of bits that resembled plastic—only Cam could eventually tell us for sure. The poor guy had mounds of samples to test. Who knew when he'd catch up?

Another group found mushy paper-like objects. We all agreed they appeared to be decomposing in a natural way.

Tyne and I found metallic bits. Although everyone gave our pieces a good look, no conclusions were voiced.

Major Craig worked on her com, while we finished eating. "Okay, I have new assignments. After this afternoon's endeavors, we should have a pretty good idea of what this area entails. We'll have a detailed discussion after dinner."

The afternoon passed in a blur.

Tyne's and my new location revealed bits of semi-decomposed vegetation under the ground cover. As we progressed, we came upon a treasure. We found a depression filled with solids. Broken bits from unknown objects fascinated. Another jigsaw puzzle to put together?

After being scrunched over all day, the walk back to the spaceship invigorated me. I hoped I'd find time for another walk this evening, and not alone.

After a quick cleanup, we gathered in the break room.

"Who'd like to start off our discussion?" asked Major Craig. "I know you'll all send reports later this evening, but I'd like to hear your opinions now, while we're all gathered."

Cam spoke, "I think the bed is a recent creation because the remnants are not fossils—they're not old enough. What I mean is they haven't disintegrated enough to have been here any length of time. Sorry, Mile, but I think you found another garbage dump."

His idea didn't excite me. However, the rest of the crew agreed with him based on their own findings.

"Why haven't we found any real fossils?" I asked.

"We actually haven't made any systematic attempt," said Major Craig. "From the start of our expedition, we've been pointed in new directions constantly so we haven't had time, and I don't like it."

No one argued with her—our situation had put all of us a little on edge. Who controlled our journey?

And then I remembered my afternoon. "How about those solids, broken bits I mean, that Tyne and I found?" I asked. "Are they a jigsaw puzzle?"

"I don't know. Let me take samples, and clean them up, and then we'll have a better idea," said Cam.

I stifled my impatience.

The formal meeting, such as it was, then ended. We sat around talking about our day and our findings. My conversation with Squid ended up quite heated, but only because he had some quite outlandish opinions on archaeology.

"I need a walk; I'll see you later, Squid." After I stood, I glanced around the break room, but no aliens occupied any table. A little odd, but I decided the Keeki had disappeared to dance in the fading light.

Squid didn't attempt to follow me, so he'd received my message.

I wandered outside and asked the security guard on the door if he'd seen any Keeki were. "I want to watch their dancing," I added.

"They walked that way," he said, pointing in the opposite direction from today's excavation.

Probably wanted a fresh view, a new area for their dancing, I decided. Not a bad idea.

Walking in the same direction, I marveled at the differences from what we'd viewed earlier today. My path took me into a slightly hillier area. The distant hills gradually became higher but not greener.

I walked and walked and listened and listened, but nowhere did I find the Keeki. Eventually I decided they'd disappeared in a direction unknown to anyone, so I returned to the ship.

The break room was crowded with humans, but no Keeki.

"Where have you been?" asked Major Craig, after she noticed me.

I sat down at her table to answer her question. "Off getting some exercise. Too much bending over dirt today."

"Who were your walking companions?" she asked, with a knowing look on her face.

"No one, actually. I went looking for the Keeki to watch them dance, but I couldn't find them based on the security guard's directions. They must've changed their minds and gone someplace else. I continued to walk, without any contact with anyone, and then I came back. You know, I don't see any Keeki here, so they must still be outside somewhere." A personal disappointment, to be sure.

Squid and Major Craig surveyed the break room. "Very unusual," agreed Squid. "There's usually a Keeki or two here by this time, especially Tyne and Mist. Their dancing is usually earlier in the evening."

Squid gave the impression their dancing ritual made his uncomfortable, but I let it go. We'd all had numerous adjustments to make on this trip.

"Well, I'm off to read for a while, and then sleep. A good day, but some downtime is required." I smiled at everyone, and left for my room.

I found a good novel, and read for far too long.

Chapter Twenty

cave discovery
experiencing
annual Kreite celebration

After a couple of cups of caffeine the next morning, I finally woke up enough to notice another strange phenomenon—no Keeki occupied the break room.

"Has anyone seen any Keeki since yesterday?" I asked, loud enough for everyone to hear. Murmurs broke out, but no one responded.

Major Craig said, "Let me try to contact them." She worked her com for a few moments, and then sat back, exasperated. "No one's answering."

Just then, Aran entered the break room. "Just the person I wanted to see," said Sylone. "Where are the other Keeki? Are they in their cabins?"

"No." The Keeki leader kept his gaze on the floor.

"Well, where are they?" Sylone asked again.

"Unknown." Aran continued to study the floor.

Had he checked all the rooms to determine the emptiness of the Keeki cabins? Why didn't he know where they were? He was their leader!

"Fine. It's time to start searching for the Keeki. Everyone, finish up your breakfast, grab your bags, and meet outside in fifteen minutes. I'll assign search parties and areas to cover, after we've gathered."

We regrouped outside in record time. Obviously, I wasn't the only one worried about the missing Keeki. No sightings last night or this morning? Highly unusual.

Squid and I had been assigned a direction to investigate, as had other pairs from our expedition. Told to report if we found any Keeki, or after two hours, we took off.

I thought two hours of walking would stretch the limits of where the Keeki probably went, but Major Craig exhibited caution.

Squid and I strode north along the edge of the ocean. The water on our right was a blue-gray, and the sand a dirty gray. Nothing caught my eye today, which was probably just as well. I needed to focus for clues as to the Keeki's whereabouts.

The stubby vegetation, on our left, reminded me of rosemary—kind of a prickly green. I wanted to go and give the plants a sniff, but Squid wouldn't appreciate my action. He was just as bad as Tyne.

Which, of course, made me think of Tyne, and my anxiety increased. Where had the Keeki gone?

Mounds on our left started to grow in height. Their arid surfaces showed off the little vegetation. Eventually, we came upon a tall opening in the side of one of the mounds. Squid pointed his flashlight around from a distance, while holding onto my arm.

"What're you doing? Let me go," I growled.

"Your reputation precedes you. No jumping inside until we get a better look."

His pronouncement was probably just as well, because I started to sweat with anticipation of a low ceiling. My claustrophobia had returned. I couldn't understand how anyone with a severe case ever coped with life.

We crept forward toward the opening, and Squid sniffed continuously. *A little delusional*, I thought. Any noxious gas might have very well been odorless.

From the outside, Squid's flashlight and mine bounced around inside the cave. "There!" I shouted. "That's a Keeki on the ground."

"Stay here, Mile. I'll call Major Craig." I wanted to rush through the entrance to see if Tyne was inside, but we backed up as Squid made his call.

Determining our coordinates, Major Craig said *Skyfall* would arrive shortly.

After the ship landed, Squid and I hung back while Sylone organized the rescue. Cam and Briny, in their environmental suits, entered first.

As we waited, the remainder of the expedition crew arrived. Depending on their location, not everyone had been picked up by *Skyfall*. Time had been of the essence for the Keeki.

Soon Cam and Briny emerged. "The Keeki seem fine—unconscious, but not in any distress. Our readings indicate the air is human compatible, but something certainly has affected the Keeki," said Cam. "They're all accounted for, except Aran, who I assume is still hiding on *Skyfall*."

Major Craig gave Cam a half-hearted reproving glance. "Okay, let's bring the Keeki out. We have only one stretcher, so let's be efficient. We'll bring them out one by one, and then transport them to the break room since our medical bay has only one bed," said Major Craig.

Briny and I kept vigil in the break room trying to monitor the Keeki's physical readings and responses.

Tyne was the first to wake. I heard a grunt, and ran over. He struggled to sit. "Tyne, wait. You've been unconscious, just take it slowly. Your biological readings are fine, you just need to rest and let the gas, or whatever it was, remove itself from your system. Do you understand what I'm saying?" I studied his face.

Tyne grabbed my hand. "Happy."

"We're all happy you're going to be okay. How do you feel?"

"Tired." He rubbed his forehead with one hand—his other still held mine. "Sit," he said.

"You want to sit up?"

He squeezed my hand, so I assumed that meant yes. Or did he want me to sit? I didn't think so, though, so I helped him rise. When his legs dangled over the edge of the table, I said, "Sit for a minute. Then we'll try getting you off the table and onto a chair."

He grabbed my hand with both of his and wouldn't let me stray—not that I wanted to. Tyne had been on my mind most of the night. Only just now did I realize how deep my concern had been.

Briny joined us. Slowly, we both helped Tyne down from the table and onto a chair. His color appeared normal to me.

The rest of the Keeki soon recovered and joined Tyne in escaping their tabletops.

After all Keeki had been revived, Major Craig asked, "So, what happened last night?"

Apparently, Tyne was now the spokesman for the Keeki, as all of his compatriots turned his way.

"*cave discovery,*
experiencing,

annual Kreite celebration."

"*Kreite*, what's that?" asked Major Craig.

"*historical research,*
experiencing,
nests in caves."

Silence enveloped the break room.

"*Kreite affirmation,*
evolving,
nests in trees."

Silence prevailed while the crew digested Tyne's kaiku. *More difficult than usual*, I thought.

"I've got it," I said. "Tyne, you have an annual ritual celebrating your history of progressing from nests in trees to nests in caves. Is that right?"

He jumped up, grabbed my shoulders, and shook me lightly.

"I'll take that as agreement," said Major Craig. "In the future, perhaps the Keeki could warn us of any other celebrations. A heads up is always nice. You wouldn't want us to worry." Mom was being tactful, but I think she was annoyed with our aliens.

Major Craig studied the Keeki before she spoke again. "Of course, there's always the issue of why you went in the cave without testing the air. And why you didn't let any expedition member know your plans. Seems Mile isn't the only impetuous one. Think about the future. Your next encounter may not be so benign."

A feeling of vindication came upon me until I realized I hadn't been complimented, but thrown in with the Keeki. Oh, well. My reputation clung like static.

Sylone turned to Aran. "Why were you not with the other Keeki last night?"

He made another one of his non-responses. I suspected his non-answers wore a little thin with Major Craig. Tyne had questions to answer when we spoke later.

"I don't know about the rest of you, but I'm hungry. A pretty stressful morning," said Major Craig. "Keeki, if you're really tired, please return to your cabins and rest. Otherwise, food is possibly in order."

The Keeki remained in the break room, and joined us for lunch.

After a suitable time, Major Craig said, "I'd like the Keeki to stay in their rooms and rest for the afternoon. You've had a stressful time. The rest of us will explore the caves you've discovered."

Murmuring broke out amongst the Keeki, so Mom added, "This is an order. We'll meet at dinnertime, and discuss our findings."

Chapter Twenty-One

markings interest
puzzle
nonogram or new?

The humans gathered outside the ship. The caves beckoned within our view since *Skyfall* had flown here to rescue the Keeki this morning.

"Cam's going to take the first sortie, and he's going to check for any residual gases. We don't want to be surprised by any that may have crept in. Especially, any that might affect humans," said Major Craig.

We plunked ourselves on the ground and waited for Cam to give the all clear.

"I still think someone is watching us," I said. "Was the Keeki gassing a species-specific test? And now we're going to be tested in another way?"

"You're being a little paranoid, Mile," said Briny. "Who else knew we were coming to this planet?"

"That's my point. They wouldn't tell us if they were testing us, would they?" I grumbled. Why was everyone ignoring my potential reality?

Holding a scanner, Cam emerged. "Everything seems clear—even for the Keeki, if they were here. All gases have dissipated."

"What did you see inside?" I asked. I urgently wanted to start moving.

"Not much. I focused on my scanning. Patience is a virtue, Mile." He started to take off his suit.

Ha, what did he know?

Major Craig laughed at Cam's statement. "Okay, everyone, I'm going to assign teams since I see three cave entrances. Meet back here in thirty minutes."

Briny and I approached the third entrance. We turned on our flashlights and made our way inside.

Since my eyes adjusted slowly to the low light level, I stayed behind while Briny strode forward. "I'm going to walk to the right and hug the wall. I think it'll be easier for us to navigate that way rather than stumbling through the middle. Why don't you play your flashlight behind me? It'll help illuminate my passage. Then start after me, in about a minute, when you're ready."

"Good plan. Find something interesting, please. I have to keep up my reputation."

Briny laughed and started out. Her tentative steps echoed as she walked along the wall, and then I started my ramble.

The light from my flashlight bounced off the boring smooth brown wall. Then I pointed my flashlight to the center of our cave, but I only saw a rough floor with a few rocks strewn around.

"I've found something," said Briny. Her voice echoed her excitement.

I rushed forward and played my flashlight towards her beam. The wall was a lighter shade of brown, almost tan. Briny had found deep scratches, similar to ones previously encountered.

"Another puzzle for you, Mile. I know you love them." Briny smiled. "Okay, I don't know if it's a puzzle, but it's certainly something to figure out. Let's take lots of pictures."

"How far along the wall do the markings go?" I asked.

"We'll find out."

Another not terribly bright question, on my part.

Briny and I discussed how to take pictures in order to pull each piece of the inside wall together in one large diagram, but it turned out we'd worried for naught.

As we walked along and recorded the wall, I said, "This repeats. Really, I think there're only four different drawings."

"Oh, I think you're right. I never realized that, but I truly hadn't been studying the markings," said Briny. "However, we should continue and take a look at the entire surface. Who knows if a brand new picture might appear?"

So that's what we did, with the occasional perusal of the jumbled center.

"We need to make a map of what we're finding—dimensions and all. Should we go back to the entrance and start again?" I asked.

"No need. I've got my tracker app turned on. We'll get a drawing of our wanderings when we're finished," said Briny.

"Tracker app?"

"Yes. Software that tracks our progress. Since we're walking the inside walls, we should get an accurate representation. And every time I took a picture, I noted it on the app. So we can match things up with map I'll get."

Now that was handy. I needed to investigate other available software.

Briny and I continued our study of the inside wall, and then found ourselves back where we entered the cave.

"I guess our exploration is over," I commented, a little let down. "Our time is pretty much up anyway. We need to join the others."

We walked outside, and took a moment to adjust to the sunlight. After I glanced over the landscape, I spied a treasure trove of chests.

In the distance, Squid leaned over one and put out his hand.

"Don't do that!" I yelled. "You might get gassed."

Everyone, within hearing of my statement, started laughing.

"Cam's already done his testing," said Squid. "It's perfectly safe."

Well, at least my error had been on the side of caution, this time. "Well, show me what's inside, then. I'm dying of curiosity." I needed the attention off me.

Squid opened the chest he crouched in front of and started pulling out objects. Only then did I notice a couple of other chests had already been opened and their contents piled on the ground.

I turned my attention back to the items in front of Squid and me. Small, square plates, etched with marks, grabbed my interest. Then I noticed the sides of the plates weren't exactly even. They had various small amounts cut out or added.

"What are those strange little bits?" I asked. "The parts marring the edges. You know the out-and-in stuff." A thought niggled at my brain.

No one commented.

"Since we're all here, let's carry everything back," said Major Craig. "Then we can start speculating."

We grabbed up the chests and their contents, and took them to the ship. I looked forward to our discussions.

After exploring dusty caves, I enjoyed my much needed cleanup. Eventually, I joined the Keeki and humans in the break room.

Anticipating the Keeki need for information, after having been cooped up all day, Major Craig said, "Everyone, finish your dinners and we'll have a meeting."

A rush of cleanup ensued. Our meeting should prove interesting—I'd heard a few very pertinent discussions over dinner.

"Okay, who wants to start?" asked Major Craig, getting everyone's attention.

Briny raised her hand, and my mother nodded at her to go ahead. "The cave Mile and I explored had its inside walls covered with markings. We took pictures and my app made a map." Briny sent everyone the diagram, and then continued, "The markings repeated many times as we traversed the inside wall. The center of the cave only consisted of rubble—at least, what we could determine in the gloom."

"*markings interest,*
puzzle,
nonogram or new?" asked Tyne.

"I really don't know what we found, Tyne," said Briny.

"Print out the markings, Briny. Multiple copies, please. Something for our puzzlers to work on," said Major Craig. She turned to Squid. "Please report on what you and I found."

"In our cave, the walls were blank. However, the center of the cave contained five chests filled with plates. Really interesting ones." Squid pulled out his com. "I'm sending some pictures."

Major Craig gave the crew a moment to digest the new information, and then asked, pointing to the third team, "Cam?"

"We also found chests and plates, but nothing else." Cam sent us his pictures. "These plates are similar to the others, but I don't think they're identical."

What did all these plates mean?

Then my mother had an interesting idea. "The wall markings Briny and Mile found are probably a puzzle like a nonogram. However, I think the plates are a huge jigsaw puzzle."

The murmuring began, as we studied the plate pictures.

Major Craig got our attention again. "Does anyone have anything else to discuss?" After no takers, she said, "Let's put a few tables together and see what we get. We have lots to work on tonight."

A couple of people started to work on the markings Briny and I found, but the rest of us dug into the plates. In addition to regular puzzles, I loved physical puzzles like jigsaws. At the moment, I questioned my mother's theory that our recently discovered plates constituted a jigsaw puzzle, but I needed more information before I could dissent.

We worked away and I was quickly proven wrong. We'd cut around the pictures of the plates so we could try and place them together and, in the end, the jigsaw puzzlers created a picture. Various theories abounded, and I subscribed to the Milky Way fantasy, but who knew?

"I've got it," said Squid, interrupting our discussions.

"Got what?" I asked. Some days he really annoyed me.

"Your markings are another location." He'd been working on the markings Briny and I had found inside our cave.

"A little boring, Squid," I said.

After seeing his crestfallen look, I added, "Sorry. I was hoping for an exotic pole dancer, or something in that vein."

Squid, and the majority of the humans in the break room, appreciated my humor—although I suspected my mother didn't approve.

"You're really funny," said Squid. And this time I thought he meant his words.

"I'm going to the bridge and run these numbers by Major White. I'll be right back," said Squid.

We continued piecing together the jigsaw puzzle until Squid returned with Major White.

"So? No pole dancers?" I asked. A couple of laughs came my way.

"Not at all, Cadet Carter," replied Major White. "However, we have another location on Wyre to explore. Or, perhaps, are being invited to explore."

His words made us pause, and gave emphasis to my theories. "Major Craig, is that our project for tomorrow?" I asked.

Sylone smiled. "Not at all. Tomorrow we're going to the North Pole, and it's not even Christmas."

Conversations exploded, and the Keeki studied us like our minds had developed a strange disease.

"The northernmost continent is covered with ice and snow—at least, most of it. It's time to expose the Keeki to our snow roots."

The murmuring increased.

"Tomorrow will be a day of exploration—a day of personal exploration on a frozen surface. However, I'm going to limit you to using snow shoes. Skiing and tobogganing are too dangerous for a first time on a new world. If you happen to find unexplained items or unexplored caves, or, whatever else there may be, just be sure to let me know. Consider tomorrow a hybrid day—part day off, part exploration." Major Craig studied the room. "I know you're all up to the challenge."

Chapter Twenty-Two

strange devices
query
producing webbed feet?

A bundle of impatient expedition members gathered in the break room while the ship relocated to the northern continent. Cam produced snow shoes, and he started to outfit the crew.

"*strange devices,*
query,
producing webbed feet?" asked Tyne.

I had to laugh at Tyne's kaiku. A race descended from a bird-like species would certainly notice the webbing.

"Do you have snow; I mean flakes of water, making a ground cover on Keeki?"

Tyne thought for a moment. "Warm."

"Your planet is too warm for snow?" Was that what he tried to say?

"Unusual," responded Tyne.

So they had little ice and snow. The continent we were going to explore today should then be an experience for the Keeki. *How well will they cope*?

"Let's see if I can explain." How much detail would the Keeki need? Glancing around, I recognized that our conversation was being followed by everyone.

"Okay. Many areas of Earth are very cold. Water droplets from the sky, also known as precipitation, change form because of the cool temperatures. The droplets become frozen. Frozen water can take many forms. Soft frozen water is called snow. Hard frozen water is called ice." I studied the Keeki and saw some understanding of my explanation.

"We use these contraptions—they're called snow shoes—to help us walk on snow. They give a sturdier base so we don't slip and fall as often." The Keeki still seemed to be with me, so I said, "Strap them over your normal foot coverings."

I had to use the words foot coverings as the Keeki wore strange looking shoes.

Cam helped the Keeki tie on their snow shoes, and then they tried to walk. Much laughter emerged from everyone—even the Keeki.

"Okay, guys. They're really meant for outside, not in the break room. When we arrive, you can try to walk on the snow with your own shoes, but I bet you'll soon put your new snow shoes on."

I received no response other than the Keeki taking off their snow shoes. I hoped that was only for ease of walking while inside. Our day trip should be interesting, to say the least.

Skyfall shook a little during its descent. Everyone stayed in their seats.

Major Craig entered the break room immediately after our landing, and said, "Don't forget your sunglasses; it's very bright out there." She glanced at the Keeki, and I knew what she thought—I'd never seen the Keeki don protection from the sun, either.

"We've landed on a plateau. After everyone is out and ready for their day, Major White is going to relocate the ship to the bottom of this hill. It'll be a good long walk down from the plateau to the ship. Please break up into groups of three or four. I want no one alone today. We're exploring the unknown, so make sure your coms are on, in case of any emergencies."

Tyne and I began to search for a compatible teammate but before any success, Aran approached us. "Join me?" he asked.

With no tactful way to say no—Aran *really* didn't show up under my favorite person's column—the three of us started off.

Aran and Tyne soon put on their snowshoes when they found walking tough going. After a short distance from our level landing spot, their shoes had proven unsuitable.

"Where do you think we should explore?" I asked. The three of us surveyed the horizon. Various easy paths, down a gently sloping hill, caught my attention, but no landmark.

Then Tyne pointed to my right.

"What do you see? What do you want to investigate?" I asked.

"Crevasse."

I peered again at the indicated area. The color of the ice appeared a little darker, so perhaps there was a crevasse. I suspected Keeki eyes were better than ours, and since I nothing else caught our attention, I agreed with Tyne's suggestion.

We walked toward the darkness. The Keeki were pretty slow, getting used to their snowshoes. Of course, snowshoes didn't make for quick walking for anyone, at any time.

Our stroll took longer than anticipated. We slowed at numerous points to take samples of rocks and ice, and the little vegetation we found. Mostly, I took time looking at the vistas.

For obvious reasons, *Skyfall* had landed first on a large, flat plateau. And from that spot, the view was spectacular. We were on the side of a mountain, with a gentle slope easing away from us.

However, across the frozen valley, high snow-covered peaks soared. The sharp tops appeared twice as high as our plateau, and cliffs and valleys abounded.

What would this vista look like in the summer months? Would a lot of greenery appear, or would my view still be of North Pole-like surroundings?

Tyne gave me a nudge, so we continued our walk.

Eventually, we came upon a large flat area overlooking Tyne's crevasse. Since the area contained smooth flattened rocks devoid of ice or snow, I suggested a lunch break. Tyne and I sat down on one of the flat rocks, but Aran remained standing.

"Have a seat," I said, gesturing to our rock.

"Quiet time," Aran responded, and pointed to another flat area about a hundred feet away.

I couldn't tell him not to go, as he was the leader of the Keeki, but Major Craig had wanted us to stay together. On the other hand, a little privacy wouldn't hurt.

Aran wandered off, as Tyne and I watched.

After a moment's long silence, I turned to Tyne. "We need to talk about our relationship—where we're going with it."

Tyne gave me a look I thought implied exasperation.

"What's wrong?" My heart rate increased, and my mood plummeted.

"*sweetness, calmness,*
enjoying,
each other's company."

Oops, perhaps I was rushing our situation. "Yes, you're right. We're certainly enjoying each other's company. Maybe it's time to explore our cultures. I know so little about yours." How could I do that and, perhaps, back off a little?

I reached up and stroked Tyne's cheek, and then our lunches were forgotten.

A noise interrupted our cuddling—Aran had returned.

"*nature day,*
exploration,
continue to learn," said Aran.

"Yes, yes. We need to get on with our exploration. Let's pack up and take a look at Tyne's crevasse. It's right over there," I said, pointing to the dark mark.

We put our snowshoes back on, and started walking.

Close to the edge of the crevasse, we stopped to reconnoiter. I'd expected a sharp drop to the bottom but, much to my surprise, a gradual slope eased away from us. Not gradual enough for snowshoes, but certainly not as steep as expected. At the bottom, I spied a narrow flat area. For some reason, a river had come to mind, but I realized my notion was nonsensical at this altitude.

"Too bad we can't get down there," I said. "I think I see sparkly bits."

"Imagination," said Tyne.

"Perhaps, you're right. I do like to…"

Then I found myself sliding sideways down the slope. Coming to a stop at the bottom, my head thumped a rock. A little buzzed, I slowly raised my body to a sitting position. *How can I return to the top of the hill?*

Then I decided the rock had given me a concussion because a large bird came into view. We'd never previously encountered any birds on this planet—or on any of the other planets, for that matter—so the flying object must be a figment of my head bump.

My brain is messed up, that bird has Tyne's face. Then my eyesight cleared.

Tyne landed beside me. "You can fly?" I asked. "Did you jump?" My thought processes were still jumbled.

"*sweet person,*
peril,
jumping to rescue," said Tyne, with a wide Keeki grin.

Aran peeked over the top of the slope so, instead of the cuddling I needed, I told Tyne my concerns. "I think Aran pushed me."

He studied me, for a moment. Then, without another word, he rummaged in my pack, and pulled out my com. "Call."

Although he didn't comment on my suspicion, he had the right idea.

"Major Craig, we have a situation," I said, after I made contact.

"And what would that be?"

"Well, somehow, I fell down part of the mountain. And I'm not sure how to get back up. I'm okay, but perhaps someone could throw down some ropes or something so Tyne and I can be pulled up and out."

"Are you hurt?"

"Just my ego and a little head bump."

Mom laughed—in relief, I suspected. "We'll get into details later. Where are you?"

"Can you get a ping from Aran's com? He's at the top of the slope beside a nice flat area. Wide enough for the ship, I'd imagine." I sighed and said, "Ah, I think Aran pushed me."

"Wait." She went away for a few moments.

"Okay, we've got his signal. And, you're right; the area looks large enough for *Skyfall*. We'll be there shortly. Be patient." Major Craig rang off.

My middle name didn't include patience, but I decided to work on some. "Tyne, can you fly up, like you did down here?"

He shook his head. "Minimal."

"Then you get to wait with me. *Skyfall* is on its way. Why don't you tell Aran what's happening. Maybe send him a message."

The two of us found a bare rock, so we sat and clasped hands. At this point in our relationship, speaking wasn't always necessary, but I had words I wanted to articulate. Before I had a chance, we heard a yell.

We stood and looked up, and my phone rang. "Mile, always in trouble," said Cam.

"Yes, that seems to be so, oh favorite scientist of mine. Going to get Tyne and me out of here?"

"Right away. We're going to send down rescue ropes, so if you would move to the right—Tyne's right, that is—you won't get hit by them."

The ropes turned out to contain harnesses, so Tyne and I quickly returned to the top of the slope. I had the image of a backwards toboggan ride.

Major Craig said, “Okay, everyone, back into the ship. We’re going to relocate to base for the evening.”

Dinner time came none too soon.

“So, Mile,” said Cam, “causing trouble again, I see. How do you always seem to fall off things?”

I ignored him, but glanced at my mother. “I do have some ideas on how this happened but, in the meantime, tell me how everyone’s day went. Any exciting discoveries?”

Apparently, lots of fun in the snow was had by all, but no discoveries of a puzzling or scientific nature.

As the Keeki quietly disappeared, I said, “I think I’ll go out for a short walk. My fall down the slope has stiffened me up.”

“Maybe Briny should take a look at you,” said my mother.

“I’ll be fine. I just need to move around—I’m not getting any younger, you know.” I had stiffened, but the Keeki were my main concern.

Laughter followed me out of the break room—the hoped for outcome.

Exiting our ship, Sam, the posted guard, pointed to his left. Apparently my habits weren’t a secret to anyone because Tyne waited, a few yards away.

“Dancing tonight?” I asked.

“*dangerous conditions,*
threat,
slippery for everyone.”

The ice and snow would indeed make dancing a bit challenging—especially with the antics the Keeki got up to.

“So, why are you outside tonight?” I asked.

“God talking,” said Tyne.

“May I watch?” I had no idea what *god talking* was, but I wanted to learn about their culture.

“Join?” asked Tyne.

“I don’t know what to do.” I had no idea about their religion, or religions. I still hadn’t quizzed my mother about the Keeki, or even talked to Mist, for that matter.

Tyne took my hand and pulled me over to where the other Keeki waited. We all joined hands and lifted them high. The vestigial wings showed clearly and were a gorgeous range of colors with the fading sunlight bouncing up from the ice remnants and shining upon the thin film.

After a few moments, we joined our right hands in a stack, and meditated. I didn't know what else to call the ceremony.

Finally, we all put our arms around the waists beside us, and meditated for the final time. I admit I sneaked a few peaks at the Keeki but, for the most part, I joined in the meditation.

Tyne gave me a little shake to indicate the end of the service, or whatever it was.

The other Keeki took off for the ship, but Tyne stood quietly beside me

"I need you to explain more about your religions," I said. "That way I can perhaps understand what happened here this evening. Take a walk?"

Tyne put his arm around my waist, and we strolled off.

We did discuss a few topics but, mostly, we managed some major personal time.

Chapter Twenty-Three

wondrous sights
exploring
unknown and unsure

"Where did you go last night, Mile?" asked Cam.

"I needed exercise. Remember I told everyone I had stiffened up from my clumsy fall."

Cam's face smirked, but I ignored him. I certainly wasn't going to reveal *god talking* until the Keeki gave their okay, but keeping secrets in a small group often proved difficult.

"What's happening today, Major Craig?" I asked, diverting Cam's attention.

"We have a new area to explore. We'll be moving to the area specified in the last deciphered nonogram. According to Major White, the location is much warmer and drier, so no snowshoes required."

The Keeki probably weren't the only ones relieved. My harrowing day made me want to avoid cold, for a long time.

Major White's analysis of the environment turned out to be spot on. We set down on a land mass surrounded by large rocks and sand dunes. The dunes appeared to us as solid sand hills crisscrossed with paths. A lack of blowing dust helped our comfort.

Tyne and I paired up with Mist and Squid. I suspected Major Craig wanted away teams to be larger from now on. Perhaps to keep an eye on me? *Why am I the only one trouble finds?* Aran figured prominently, in my opinion. In particular, I decided to keep Aran in front of me where he'd always be visible.

The four of us walked in the direction Major Craig had indicated for our away team—north-west as indicated by the map finder on my com.

We walked upon firmly packed ground. Not really a designated path but comfortable, flat, and free of obstacles like rocks and pebbles, and vegetation.

"I think we should go around that hill that's coming up," said Squid. "Before we start climbing, let's see what's around the back. We might find a fairyland, or a lake, or a deep depression, or…"

"We get the point," I said. "Tyne, Mist, what do you think?"

"*wondrous sights,*

exploring,

unknown and unsure," said Tyne.

I thought I'd caught onto Tyne's thought processes, and then he throws a kaiku at me I didn't understand. So I decided to go with the *wondrous sights* comment—in a positive way, of course.

"Okay, Squid, lead on. Find something new, something other than a puzzle to intrigue us."

Although Squid gave me a dirty look, he didn't respond verbally. He turned around and took off in a brisk manner. So we hustled to catch up. Another one of my conversational gaffes, I decided.

The four of us followed a flat path circumnavigating the bottom of the hill. I marveled at its smoothness. I suspected man-made, or alien-made to be more precise, but no markings proved my supposition.

"This area has no plant or animal life," I said. "Has anyone seen any?" Maybe I'd missed the indicators.

No one responded, so I asked, "Did anyone see any life yesterday, up in the snow fields?"

"No," said Squid. "Our whole trip has been remarkably biologically free. Tyne?"

"*missing water,*

wind,

absence of life."

"Do you mean the lack of water and wind means life would have a hard time thriving?" I asked. My recent experiences made me decide I'd never be a linguist—at least one dealing with alien tongues.

"No life-force," said Tyne.

Did the Keeki need wind in order to survive? Did they dance to create a breeze?

"Hurry up!" yelled Squid, who'd gotten ahead. "I see something."

We ran to catch up, and discovered Squid's surprise.

"Another pyramid?" I asked. "This isn't the first time we've encountered a pyramid on our expedition." We all remembered the one on Needles where I'd received my second gassing.

The back part of the pyramid nestled into the side of the hill. Although similar in size to the Needles pyramids, this one was alone and devoid of dust, markings, and ridges on its outside surface.

"So, what are we going to do?" I asked. "Anyone have any ideas? Are we going to look inside?" We all stared at the one entrance. Major Craig hadn't designated an away team leader, so we needed to make a group decision.

No one commented, so I said, "One pyramid, by itself, seems strange. Why don't Tyne and I go to the left, and you guys walk to the right. We'll meet up on the back side of the hill. It shouldn't take us long to traverse around, and then we can decide what to do next. I do think we need to explore at least a little before we call Major Craig."

With no objections voiced, we paired and took off.

Tyne and I didn't speak. I wanted to spend my time studying my surroundings and I was sure Tyne wanted to do the same.

The hillside turned out to be covered with many crisscrossing paths. "Tyne, do you think we should wander up one of those paths? I'm sure we could take a few moments before meeting Squid and Mist."

****

The next I knew Tyne's arms grabbed me, and he pulled me up into a sitting position. I glanced at the grungy floor and rubbed my face. Apparently, I'd been lying on it for some time, given the residue my face transferred to my hand.

"Tyne, where are we?" Almost immediately I recognized my nonsensical question. How would he know?

He continued to grip me.

"I'm terribly thirsty. What happened?" Another question he wouldn't be able to answer; my brain must really be addled.

I rummaged in my pack for my water bottle while I studied my surroundings. We were ensconced in a fairly small room. Four doors broke the monotonous walls, and nothing resided on the floor—other than us and the grit.

Tyne helped me to my feet, and I took a gulp of water. “Another room, another mystery. That’s the story of our lives.”

I studied the four doors; each with a different color. “So, Tyne, what’s your favorite color? Why don’t you pick a door and we’ll be adventurous. Maybe we’ll emerge back on Wyre.”

Chapter Twenty-Four

pictures, samples
acquire
study for details

What color would Tyne pick? I didn't think it would really matter, or would it? Other than four differently colored doors, our prison offered little information.

"*red lucky,*
decisions,
conflicted and confused."

On Tyne's face, I did detect confusion—most likely about our whole situation, I suspected.

"Lucky red door it is." The only interpretation I wanted to take from his words.

The two of us walked across the room, but then we hesitated. After exchanging glances, Tyne reached out and turned the door handle. I followed him, and the door shut behind us with a loud click. So I tried the door knob—locked. *We might be in here for a while. Is this a new prison cell?.*

This red-doored room appeared smaller than the previous one. The walls were a drab brown and lacked any additional color or markings. A mound of objects, in the middle of the floor, caught our attention.

I started forward, but Tyne grabbed my arm.

"*pictures, samples,*
acquire,
study for details."

From a distance of ten feet, we studied the mound and took pictures. Then we walked closer to take samples. What else would members of a scientific expedition do?

Then I confirmed my suspicions—we'd found a pile of jigsaw puzzle plates. Tyne and I rummaged about on the floor, and started to put the puzzle together.

A pretty easy one this time. The drawings on the plates made the matchups easy. The lack of dust did make me wonder how long this puzzle had been here.

"Okay, that wasn't so hard. What do you think this is, Tyne? A map of something?" Swirls radiated from a center blob. The swirls tapered off to single points.

"*star system,*
reflecting,
points of light."

"You think this is an artistic impression of a star system?" I recognized an abstract drawing, but I had no clue as to its meaning. How had Tyne come to his conclusion?

"*lights design,*
recognizing,
Keeki home system."

"This is your home?" Was that what he said?

"Yours," said Tyne, with a big smile.

"You think this is *our* solar system?" No wonder he sported a big smile.

Tyne made a gesture of affirmation, so I took a picture of our final result and ran it through software on my com.

"You're correct, Tyne. Smart analysis. Now why would a picture of our solar system be on a puzzle?" And in the middle of nowhere, I might add. The uncertainty of our situation troubled me more than I could express.

With no idea how to proceed, I tried to call my mother, but my com had no reception.

Then a loud click impinged upon the silence. I twirled around, and asked, "Was that the door?"

Tyne jerked around toward the door, and I trailed behind him. The door opened for us, and we entered our original room. At least, the red door hadn't exited into a brand new location.

My body's discomfort grew. "You know, I'm going to need a washroom pretty soon. How're we going to handle that?"

We both studied our original room, but nothing new had appeared. The room was as empty as ever. *What am I going to do?*

Then a whining noise, like a transporter, made both of us glance around to find the source. We realized one corner of our jail now sported a small room.

"What's, what's…"

Another noise and we both swirled around to notice a second corner now contained a two-stack of what we could only classify as beds.

"Tyne…" Before I had a chance to add to my words, a large table and chairs appeared in the third corner.

Anxiously, we both stood still, but nothing else appeared. I said, "I'm going to check out the little room."

Tyne hovered as I walked over and opened the door. "Okay, we have a rudimentary washroom. This's good." I shooed Tyne away and used the facilities.

Afterwards, I joined Tyne at our new table. "You know, I sure could use some food and drink. It must be about lunchtime, although I have no idea of where we even are, let alone the local time."

Once again a noise interrupted our conversation, and a table appeared in the final empty corner. I walked over, and then said, "My wishes keep coming true. Tyne, we've got food and water. You must eat." He joined me and we gathered sustenance and proceeded to the big table.

Should I ask our captors to let us return to our expedition? Somehow I didn't think my request would be honored. We'd been brought here for a reason—an unknown reason—and I didn't think we'd accomplished all of our tasks yet.

We finished our silent lunch and returned our dishes to the food table.

"I think we're going to be here for a while, Tyne. Shall we investigate another door?"

We'd had no indication our captors had planned any other activities.

Chapter Twenty-Five

performing challenges
accepting
understanding of captors

Tyne didn't respond to my words, but simply started walking in the direction of the yellow door. With no idea why that particular color had caught his fancy, I decided one unknown was as good as another.

The door opened easily, and we walked into what I could only describe as a dead end hallway.

I took a closer look at the three light brown walls, and then touched the surface of the one on my right.

Tyne growled, probably for good reason considering my recent inclinations, but I didn't care. All barriers were down, as far as I was concerned, since we'd been abducted against our wills.

The right hand wall was slightly rough and its temperature was neutral. No particles flaked away after my hand strokes. The left hand wall was of a similar texture.

Although the far end of the hallway was a blank wall, the two side walls sported openings—entrances tall enough to walk through, I estimated. The dark interior revealed nothing about their natures.

Naturally, the yellow door locked behind us. "Now, what are we supposed to do? Pick one of these two new doorways?" Were we going to start going in circles and get lost? Would we find our expedition members through one of the openings? Or had we been transported to another world?

Tyne interrupted my negative musings.

"*performing challenges,*
accepting,
understanding of captors."

Again Tyne had correctly deduced our options—we had none. "Okay, lead on."

After receiving his *look*, I said, "Pick an opening; an adventure waits." I sighed. Not too adventurous, I hoped with all my heart. This expedition had already provided too much excitement—at least for me.

Tyne picked a doorway, random I assumed. A thought popped into my mind—*I don't want adventure, I want a romantic interlud*e. However, my wants needed to wait.

With much reluctance, I walked through the opening Tyne chose, and we came upon another long hallway. Again an opening further down each side was noticeable because light from somewhere shone onto the passageway. A third opening was visible at the end of the passageway—unlike the previous hallway.

"What's this all about? Do we have to choose one of these doors on the side walls, or do we continue straight ahead?" Our choices had begun to mount. What if we got lost?

Tyne bent down and picked up something at the foot of the nearest opening.

"*interesting clues,*
searching,
possibly discover treasures."

He passed me the item he'd found on the floor.

"Tyne, this is a piece of a jigsaw puzzle. Look," I said. I shoved it in his face.

Tyne smiled and grabbed my other hand and gave it a kiss.

Apparently, he forgave me for being awkward. "I'm going to put this in my pack. Who knows what else we're going to find?" Then a notion popped into my thoughts. "Tyne, are there more of these puzzle pieces at the other openings?"

Tyne gave me a quick grin. He didn't let go of my hand so I had little choice but to follow. We deposited additional pieces in my backpack.

Thinking back on his kaiku, I focused on his words.

A treasure hunt? Maybe more clues would surface as Tyne suggested. "How are we going to keep track of our path, with all these choices to make? We might want to return to our starting point—our room with the facilities."

Tyne held up his com.

"You're right, we could use the GPS. Let me see if it works in here." I fumbled about, but I found no reception.

"No go. We'll have to think up something else," I said.

Tyne studied our surroundings, and then walked up to one of the doorways. He took a wide marker out of his pack and wrote on the side of the opening.

I peered at his scribble, but I didn't know what it meant. "What did you write?"

"Number."

"We're going to mark the openings! That's brilliant. I think I'll make a map as we go along. So what number did you write? One?"

His head motion agreed with me, so I started a map on my com. Very crude, but it might help us in the end—whatever the ending turned out to be.

Then a brilliant notion came to mind so I rummaged in my pack. "Tyne, I think I'm going to also leave one of my stones here on the floor as a marker. What do you think? Your mark on the wall might disappear, or something."

He laughed, picked up my stone, and wrote the same number on it.

An excellent use for my stones, I decided, and reinforced my collecting. Of course, will I ever have another opportunity?

The opening Tyne chose led to a new corridor. Of course, this corridor also had two openings on each side wall, but none on the end. Each of the doorways had a ruler leaning against it.

Ruler may not have been the correct description. I picked up the nearest one. The object was fairly long, about three feet I estimated, with a width similar to the jigsaw puzzle pieces we'd previously encountered. One long side was perfectly straight, while the other had indentations.

"Tyne, I think we should pick up those objects leaning at the openings. They might be useful, later."

"Agreed."

So we gathered up the four rulers and put them in our packs. Because of their length, they stuck out the top. Something like lettering caught my eye, but I'd study it later.

"Which door are you going to pick this time?" I asked Tyne.

"Closest." He pulled me to him and rubbed one of my ears.

"Okay," I said, trying to catch my breath. I knew we needed to continue our journey, but the effort required to focus was monumental.

The next corridor contained six exits. "Now what are we going to do?" I asked.

Tyne laughed and pulled a small item out of one of his pockets, and threw it on the floor. Then he picked it up and presented it to me.

I peered at the many-sided object and the mark where Tyne's finger pointed.

"What's this? What does that mark mean?"

"*ingle*."

Seeing the look on my face, he said,

"*small object,*

rolling,

choice of randomness."

Then the light dawned. "This is like an eight-sided die, and the mark is a number." I grinned. "So we can choose which door to take?"

"Understanding," said Tyne.

I laughed. "So which door did the *ingle* choose? And I think we'd better continue making marks of our own on the doorways we choose."

Tyne led me to his random doorway, and through we went into another drab corridor.

This time, four tiny doors and one large enough for us to walk through appeared. The walls remained consistent.

"Tyne, now what are we going to do?" I glanced at him. He didn't answer. One too many surprises today, I suspected.

"Okay, how about we open one of the little doors and see what's inside?" We needed to continue.

Tyne pointed at one, so I bent down. A small handle caught my attention, so I pulled on it. Possibly too adventurous, but I was beyond caring.

The door opened, and a puzzle piece lay on the floor of a small enclosed box. The only item visible, I picked it up and showed it to Tyne. "What do you think this's for?"

"Save," he said, pointing to my backpack.

He hadn't answered my question, but I simply said, "Sure. How about we check the other small doors?"

So we did, and came up with three more items looking remarkably like corner pieces of a jigsaw puzzle.

"More items to save, I guess." I decided not to ask for his opinion on their usefulness.

Tyne didn't speak, but he did point to my pack.

I stuffed the new items inside, and then said, "I guess it's on to the door we can actually go through."

Tyne grabbed my hand and pulled me through.

This time we exited into a hallway that consisted of ten tiny doors—five on each side wall—and one humanoid-sized door at the end of the corridor.

"More bits and pieces, I presume. What do you think?"

"*found items,*
acquiring,
onward the adventure."

Easy for Tyne to say. "Well, I think this is the end of my adventure. If that door at the end of the hallway doesn't lead back to our room, or *Skyfall*, for that matter, I'm going to sit down and refuse to move."

My statement shocked Tyne. He stared at me, but said nothing.

This isn't getting us anywhere. "Let's open up those ten doors and see what's inside. After that we'll go through the big door and see what happens." After that, I promised nothing.

Thankful for something to do, Tyne agreed. We gathered an item from behind each door.

"You know, Tyne, some of these objects look like spaceships. And I think we have a wormhole, maybe a solar system, stuff like that." Not puzzle pieces that was for sure.

"*unusual items,*
indicating,
objects of interest."

His kaiku didn't give me much information, but I thought it was at least a confirmation of my thoughts.

Then we both stood still without moving. So I said, "Tyne, much as I'd like to spend time here with you, I think we need to go through the big door."

"Affirmative," said Tyne, before stroking my cheek.

And the big door returned us to our starting point, the yellow door.

"Oh, we're back! I'm so happy. Tyne?"

He grabbed me and we hugged. Although together all day, returning to a bit of normalcy cheered us. Although, I had to admit, our normalcy was unusual.

And I ruminated on our day. I used to like mazes, but my feelings now turned in the opposite direction.

"Well, I'm glad to be back. I need food and fluid and a wash up, not necessarily in that order." Perhaps the stress of our day contributed, but I babbled. I turned to the restroom and disappeared for a time. After I returned, food had appeared. Somebody, or something, obviously listened to our conversations.

I started eating and glanced at my watch. "I don't know if my time is correct," I said, "but I think we were out in the maze for many hours. Must be why I feel so tired."

"*long day,*
frustrating,
time to relax."

I hoped Tyne was suggesting *together time*.

Chapter Twenty-Six

current situation
frustrating,
personal happiness conflicted

The next morning, we discovered dishes of food on our sustenance table. After pointing out the situation to Tyne, he investigated while I washed up.

After we started eating, Tyne reached over and rubbed my ear. I smiled, and fond thoughts echoed through my mind. "Happy?" I asked, finally.

"*current situation,*
frustrating,
personal happiness conflicted."

I couldn't argue—I wanted out of our situation as much as he did. Why were we being held captive? Why were the two of us being held and tested away from the others? What had happened to the rest of our expedition?

"Let's get this over with, Tyne. I suspect we have two more doors to explore. Which one next?"

He pointed at the black door, so off we went and discovered nothing. Well, we found an empty room. Walls devoid of anything except black paint, and an empty floor, greeted us. *Now what're we supposed to do?*

Before I obsessed about our situation, a table, chairs, paper, and writing utensils appeared.

Tyne and I scooted over and took a look. After a quick glance, we came to the same conclusion—the new table held eight nonograms.

"Whoever's subjecting us to these tests must think we're good at deciphering nonograms." Our next step eluded me.

"*leaving clues,*
abductors,
situation to challenge."

"Well, I don't know what kind of clues our abductors have left for us. What're they trying to say? The maze was just weird, although we did pick up a few items. Were those clues? If so, I have no idea what they're for. Do you?"

Tyne shook his head.

"However, I think you're correct. These nonograms have been sent to us for some reason. We'd best get busy." Frustrating, but our abduction hadn't been boring so far.

We settled at our new table and studied the eight pieces of paper. "Tyne, I think the paper and pens are wipe-off."

He gave me a strange look, so I said, "I mean, if we make a mistake it will be easy to erase any marks we want to with these tissues." I pointed to a pile of fluff, and picked up one. Then I filled in a square on one of the puzzles, and proceeded to wipe it off. "See. Easy to correct any mistakes."

Tyne perked up. He grabbed one of the puzzles and started working. Of course, that was my cue to be productive.

A companionable and quiet morning resulted. Tyne and I both loved puzzles, so our endeavor pleased us.

After around three hours of puzzle solving, a noise distracted us. Glancing around, another table had appeared. And shortly, thereafter, food.

"Thank goodness," I said. "I didn't realize how long we've been working. I'm dying of thirst and hungrier than I expected."

We took a welcome break. While we ate, Tyne thrust one of the nonograms under my nose.

"What?" Why did he act so upset?

He tapped his finger on the paper, so I took a closer look. Black dots appeared amongst the numbers on the two edges of the nonogram.

"Tyne, what do those dots mean?" The black dots gave me an inkling of why his patience had been tested.

"*represent numbers,*
unknowns,
participants to uncover."

His statement took me a moment to figure out. "The puzzle has even more missing clues? The dots represent missing numbers?"

Tyne sighed, and then gave me a hug. "Cheerfulness. Acceptance."

Okay, I'd be a cheerful little camper. Harrumph.

Another hum and washroom facilities appeared. I suspected our sojourn would continue.

We went back to the puzzle table and resumed our digging. The puzzles with dots proved to be even more difficult than I'd imagined.

We worked all afternoon and managed to complete six. Then we embarked on the last two—our final challenge. "This nonogram I have, Tyne, doesn't seem too bad. How about yours?"

"*nothing missing,*
small,
ease of convention."

I guessed his words meant his nonogram was fairly easy too. "Okay, let's have a race to see who finishes first."

Tyne smiled. "Prize?"

Such a smartass. "I'm sure I'll think of something."

We ignored each other and worked as fast as we could. Tired of this current game or test, and I was sure Tyne was too, I just wanted it over.

As luck would determine, we finished within seconds of each other. "Tie?" I asked.

"Both prizes," said Tyne, grinning.

A discussion for later, I decided. Perhaps in a personal context. "What do we have? Let's see if we can put all eight together."

With eight completed nonograms to arrange, I thought we might encounter a problem. However, the solution came together in no time.

"What do we have here, Tyne?" I asked, after agreeing on an arrangement of the eight puzzles.

"*perspective changed,*
rearranged,
our galaxy unveiled."

"You're going to have to try again. I don't know what you're saying."

Frustration appeared as Tyne searched for different words. Convinced the translator routinely garbled his kaiku, I tried to be sympathetic.

"*alien perspective,*
timeliness,
our galaxy unveiled."

Now these words I thought I understood. "Do you mean this puzzle is a representation of our own galaxy, from a different perspective and a different time other than now?"

My words weren't elegant, but Tyne understood. He walked to my side of the table and gave me a hug. Thank goodness, my personal Keeki loved physical contact.

"So what're our captors trying to say? What does this picture mean for us?"

From the look on Tyne's face, neither of us knew how to answer my questions.

Then the black door opened back into our main living quarters.

"I guess it's time to go home, Tyne."

He grinned and grabbed my hand.

Our dinner and clean clothes soon arrived so we chose to ignore my questions.

During dinner, we said little. My thoughts focused on the other ESF expedition members. In particular, how worried was my mother about our disappearance? Of course, with no idea if other disappearances had taken place, and no contact with anyone—alien or expedition—my questions would remain unanswered. Perhaps everyone was in some kind of personal hell.

My thoughts depressed me.

So after we put our dishes away on the side table, I asked, "What do you want to do this evening, Tyne? Should we investigate that last door?"

Before Tyne responded, a box plunked onto the floor in the middle of our room.

We rushed over. After looking inside, we scurried to our table, and dumped out the contents.

"Looks like a jigsaw puzzle, Tyne. I guess we're expected to put it together. Want to give it a try?"

He smiled, gave me a kiss, and sat down on the table's opposite side.

We pushed and poked pieces until none remained along. However, our puzzle was incomplete.

"Tyne, why are there gaps? Missing pieces? Why wouldn't our captors send us the complete puzzle?"

He didn't answer, but continued to study our result.

What's missing? I decided to do an analysis. I started to write a list on my com, at least that function still worked. Then Tyne interrupted my thoughts by grabbing my pack.

"Hey, that's mine, not yours." He'd obviously mixed up our backpacks.

He ignored me, and dumped the contents of my pack on my bed.

"Tyne, what're you doing? Have you lost your Keeki mind?" Should I be annoyed, concerned, amused, or infuriated?

"Missing," he said, and held up one of the pieces picked up in the maze.

I grabbed it and went over to the table.

"Tyne, this's a match! You're so smart." I grinned. "Okay, I forgive you for dumping out my pack. Bring everything you think we need over here."

Tyne gathered up puzzle pieces and the rulers from my pack. Seemed a little strange, but I didn't argue—he'd batted a thousand today.

We inserted the pieces into the puzzle. Apparently, our scavenging had proven successful—we'd completed the puzzle.

Then I looked at the rulers, and realized our puzzle needed an outline; something to hold it together.

"Tyne, can you also get the two rulers from your pack, please. I think the two of them and my two form the outside of the puzzle."

Our four rulers did indeed complete the outline.

"What's this supposed to be?" Apparently, I loved to ask unanswerable questions.

We studied the design on the puzzle, and I came up with nothing. I looked at Tyne, and saw a flushed face and tears in his eyes.

"What's wrong?" I'd never seen him this upset.

He passed a hand over his head. "Keeki system."

"This's your home?"

Tyne gave me a hug, and said,

"*system, planets,*
emotional,
missing home Keeki."

Although an orphan, Tyne still had family and friends on Keeki. I ran around the table and gave him a hug. "I know you're missing your family and acquaintances. I wonder what our captors think about Earth. Or do they think we're from the same place?"

Tyne laughed at my nonsensical statements, and then grabbed my hand and gave it a kiss. Such a romantic, and I decided not to trade him in.

"So what shall we do now that we've solved this puzzle?"

Before either of us had a chance to speculate, another box appeared on the floor.

"I guess we'd better look," I said, with some reluctance. My enthusiasm for adventure was currently at a low.

We walked over to the box and studied the outside of the plain brown cardboard-like box. So, with my reputation for being gassed unconscious, I gestured to Tyne. I didn't think he was particularly impressed with my suggestion, but he pulled the top open anyway.

He peered inside, and then picked up the box and walked to our table.

"What's in there?" I asked, scurrying after him. He grabbed my hand and wrapped me in a hug. The hug I could handle; the suspense I couldn't.

"Happy?" he asked.

"Well, except for the fact you won't let me look in the box, I'm very happy here with you." We snuggled for a bit, and then he let me go and gestured at the box.

Much to my surprise, my *Ticket to Ride* game surfaced—at least a copy of it.

"I guess we're expected to game, instead of investigating the last door. That means we'll be spending the night here, and exploring the last door tomorrow."

"Agreed," said Tyne. "Togetherness."

I loved him for his words.

"Well, two-player *Ticket To Ride* is slightly different. Let me explain." The changes were minimal, so we soon started.

I had no chance to ask Tyne about his world and culture, as he questioned me about mine.

After three games, I started to fade. "Tyne, I'm tired. I need sleep. How about you?"

"Same?" asked Tyne.

What did he mean? I thought for a moment, and his smile answered my unspoken question. "I think I can handle you—I mean sleeping in the same bed."

Chapter Twenty-Seven

water peace
companionship
day of enjoyment

The next morning, I asked, "Tyne, today must be the day we tackle the last door, the blue one. Are you up to it?"

"Wait?" A hopeful glance came my way.

He wanted to wait? Was this possible? "Sure. Perhaps we should spend the day playing *Ticket to Ride* and relaxing. No downtime recently and I need some." His idea boosted my enthusiasm for life. The last few days of uncertainty had increased my anxiety. With no idea what my future might bring, my lack of control was a concern.

Then the blue door clicked open. I glanced at Tyne and I recognized he'd also come to my conclusion. We gathered up our packs, and threw in the extra bottles of water and packaged lunches that had appeared at breakfast. Apparently, our captors had organized our day.

"Onwards and upwards," I said to Tyne, and motioned to the blue door.

He had no idea what my words meant, but Tyne pushed the door the rest of the way open, and I followed. Our feet landed on a large rocky outcropping.

Inching forward, I studied the ledge we stood upon—we overlooked a river. Quite a strange river as it started at a blank wall behind us. Tethered to a rock at my right, I caught a glimpse of a raft.

"I guess we're supposed to explore this river, Tyne."

He glanced at me, and then at the raft. Not a water person, Tyne's reluctance impacted my mood.

"I know, I know. Not very substantial looking but we do have poles for pushing the raft along, and even a rudder. Having a rudder is the best." Did Tyne understand? I couldn't read the expression on his face.

"sailboat movement,
different,
water format unusual."

He didn't understand the collection of logs at all. "Just think of the raft as a sailboat on a narrow ocean. You're used to a sailboat now, so this should be fun. We use the poles like sails, to help push our conveyance forward." I didn't really want to remind him about his experience, but I hoped Tyne would consider the raft as somewhat familiar.

Various ropes attached to the top of the raft made me suggest we tie our backpacks on. I thought about doing the same to Tyne, because of his previous dumping, but I then decided he might think I lacked confidence about his abilities.

We started off at a slow pace. The river meandered and the bright sun improved my mood. I tried to relax, but I kept thinking about how a river appeared behind a closed door—a door we'd decided not to investigate until it opened and gave us an obvious invitation or, more likely, command. Invitation or command—what was the difference, at this point?

Our trip continued at a leisurely pace as Tyne kept trying to beach us. At the beginning of our excursion, his poling left much to be desired, but in a relatively short time he began to get the hang of rafting and our path smoothed out.

The river was bounded, on both sides, by plateaus that dropped directly to the water. The dirty brown cliffs gave no information, and the tops of the plateaus were hidden from view.

How benign was this planet? Actually, after asking my question, I realized immediately I didn't even have a clue where we'd been imprisoned. Quite a depressing thought.

The occasional sandbar, or beach, intruded on the shoreline.

"water peace,
companionship,
day of enjoyment," commented Tyne, interrupting my negative thoughts.

Our moment was a first—we'd both relaxed at the same time. "Why don't we pull in over there and have some lunch? Looks like a great place to stop."

Tyne glanced at where I pointed and helped me pole to a sandbar on our right. I tied the raft to a rock, and we settled down to a peaceful meal.

"We should think of a name for our raft, Tyne. How about the *Hukeek*? You know—a
combination of *Humans and Keeki*?"

Tyne didn't deign to respond, and I didn't blame him. Water remained his least favorite choice of travel—especially when our situation was not of our own making.

After eating, we both fell asleep. Quite a surprise to me, but our last few days had been stressful. Why had we been singled out for this particular journey?

After we'd recovered, we gathered up our belongings and started down the river again. This time our path became rockier. Boulders appeared in the river—boulders we needed to avoid.

Tyne tried, but we hit a few. Being the stronger, I had a hard time adjusting to Tyne's antics—ah, maneuvering.

Then we became jammed between two large rocks, and Tyne started to slide off the raft. I caught his overall, but I had quite a struggle pulling him back on board.

"*water faster,*
rougher,
difficult to control."

After uttering his words, Tyne gasped. I didn't think he taken in too much water, but I needed to keep an eye on his physical symptoms. The Keeki most likely exhibited different reactions than humans, and I was no expert on their physiology—well, maybe just a little.

"Tyne, relax. Our raft is currently stuck between two rocks, so we're going nowhere."

He didn't appear uncomfortable, or even too unhappy, but I wanted to give him a moment to recover.

"Continue," he eventually spouted.

His voice didn't indicate enthusiasm, but what else could we do? Sit and wait for our captors?

We secured our backpacks, and then started pushing with the raft poles. Not as stuck as imagined, once the boulders released the raft, it started rushing down the river because of the increased water flow.

For about hour, we poled and bounced and had a crappy time. At least I did, and I was sure Tyne's experience was worse. *Why did our captors torture us*?

"Tyne, why don't we try to land? We need a rest break."

Studying our surroundings, I found a possible stopping point.

"Let's pole over there," I said, pointing towards a rocky beach.

Tyne glanced at my waving arm, and then nodded. However, our raft proved stubborn. Eventually, we squirmed our conveyance in the right direction.

"Looking good," I said. "We're almost there, Tyne."

We poled for a couple of moments, and then Tyne decided to jump off the raft.

"Tyne!" I yelled. I didn't really think he'd jumped—he'd lost his balance, as only Tyne could.

I frantically surveyed my surroundings, but Tyne was nowhere in sight. "What am I going to do?" I asked. "How can I save him? I don't even know where he is. Should I jump in the river?" I'd started to panic, and my words spewed into the air.

The next thing I recognized was potential bruises. We'd landed back in our captive chambers—piled together on the floor.

Shaking a non-moving Tyne, I asked, "Are you okay? Talk to me!"

He expelled water, and then said, "Interesting experience."

"Interesting experience? You almost drowned! I thought I'd lost you. Are you okay?" My emotions bounced around our room, but Tyne was alive so I tried to breathe.

He grabbed me and attempted to make my hysterics subside. I succumbed to his hugs.

"So, now what're we going to do?" Guilt consumed my thoughts. I should've been worrying about Tyne.

"Cleanup. Day long."

I couldn't argue—our day had left me definitely grungy.

So we made ourselves presentable, and relaxed at our main table. Dinner soon appeared.

Exhausted after a challenging day, we had an early night.

Chapter Twenty-Eight

necessities provided
loneliness
confusion and anger

The next morning our breakfast arrived at the usual time, but nausea threatened. Tyne pushed food around his plate, so I suspected his appetite had also disappeared.

"Well, we've run out of doors to explore. What's next?" I asked.

Tyne had no answer, other than to look at the ceiling.

What did his gesture mean? Did he think a door would open in the ceiling, or did he think someone listened to our conversation, or…?

Before I had a chance to utter a word, the Keeki Aran appeared in the middle of our main room.

"What're you doing here? Where's everybody else? Are you here to rescue us?" My words spilled out, and Tyne and I both stood.

"I am not Aran," said his body double.

"Well, you could've fooled me. Are you our captor?" Anger filled my mind. "Why do you look like a Keeki?"

Then his body changed while Tyne and I stared. Watching a body morph reminded me of all shades of horror and science fiction.

After the alien's transformation, Tyne and I continued to stand motionless, and speechless—although my shakiness made me want to collapse on the floor.

The humanoid alien exhibited five fingers and one thumb on each hand. At our distance, his skin layer appeared thicker than human. Somewhat wider eyes complimented a slightly tinged green face. The rest of the alien's physique was within normal limits for a humanoid, except for the third ear nestled within the silver hair on the top of his head.

Is this his real form? Or is this what he wants us to see?

No one spoke, so I broke the silence. "Okay, as I asked before, who are you? And why are we here?" A new alien form made me realize I should've expected a new species to eventually appear if Tyne and I survived our trials. There was no way the Keeki could've engineered Tyne's and my captivity.

Several long moments passed before the alien spoke. "I am from Similo. You may call me Rawa. You and Tyne were brought to this room for testing." Then he stopped speaking.

What kind of alien ambassador had so few words? Then I wondered whether he really was an ambassador, perhaps he was a…conqueror?

"Okay, I'll bite. Why Tyne and me? Why did you choose us for your tests?" Being a guinea pig didn't excite me.

Of course, Tyne got the usual look on his face when I uttered phrases he didn't understand—like *I'll bite.* What words had the translator given Tyne? Thank goodness, I didn't say *guinea pig* out loud.

"My requirements were one person from each race, optimally in a relationship," replied Rawa.

We did meet his criteria, but I still didn't understand why our situation had happened. "Is our testing over? I can only rescue Tyne so many times, you know."

I suspected, after my remark, Tyne pointed his evil Keeki eye in my direction, but I didn't look his way.

A new alien race would require more observation before I was sure Rawa's face contained the hint of a smile.

"Yes." Rawa put his hands on his waist, as he answered my question regarding our testing being complete.

I hated terse aliens. Okay, maybe not all—my exception list included the Keeki, of course. "What now? Do we get to go home?" I gave myself a mental slap. "What I meant is, do we get to go back to our ship? And really, we need explanations. Why this testing? Were you the one who sent us all over the galaxy investigating dead planets and solving puzzles?" I had many further questions, but I wanted a glimmer of understanding before I continued.

"A good deduction, Mileena Carter. I will explain the basis for our experiment," said Rawa. "In the beginning…"

I interrupted. "We're not the people to whom you need to give your explanations, or excuses. You need to talk to Major Craig. She's the leader of our expedition."

Rawa's face lost all emotional clues. His face had become totally impassive.

"Understood. Prepare to depart; gather your belongings." One of his hands gestured around the room.

His words had an ominous ring—what would we experience next? Would he really send us back to *Skyfall*?

We stuffed our packs with everything we could put our hands on, including *Ticket to Ride*. Then we went to stand beside Rawa. He grabbed our hands, and then we thumped unsteadily onto the break room floor.

He released our hands, and allowed us to back away from his presence.

"Mile, Tyne, where have you been?" asked Major Craig, her voice rising. "We've been looking for you everywhere." My mother wanted to rush over and hug me, but our situation was impossible.

I tried to give her a look that acknowledged her feelings because I also wanted her comfort.

"You'd better ask our new best friend, Rawa. He abducted us and decided to use us in his experiments." My crankiness had returned, and the look on Tyne's face indicated his own frustration.

Major Craig gave a hand signal, and the security personnel in the break room moved to surround Rawa.

"Really, Major Sylone Craig, relax. I can remove myself anytime, just like I transported Mile and Tyne to another place, and then brought them back," said Rawa.

We all recognized the truth of his statement.

"Okay, fine then. Let's sit down and discuss the situation. I assume that's allowed?" asked my mother.

"Do not get testy, Major Craig. I brought back your daughter and her boyfriend, without harm, so you should be happy."

The break room buzzed. The knowledge of our relationship—actually two relationships— were revelations to various portions of the crew.

"You're not the most tactful alien I've known," said Sylone. "You have a lot of explaining to do."

Rawa made a head motion, but didn't reveal his thoughts. "Of course. Where shall I begin?"

"At the beginning might be helpful," said Major Craig. Her anger had not melted away.

All personnel focused on Rawa, but I decided to break the flow before he had a chance to begin. "I need to interrupt," I said. "Where's Aran? The real Aran, I mean. Rawa, you portrayed yourself initially to Tyne and me as Aran, why did you do that?"

Rawa gave me a look anyone would interpret as exasperation. "I infiltrated your expedition many days ago. I took the form of Aran to watch your activities."

"So where *is* Aran?" reiterated my mother, as she stood. I suspected she wanted to shake a fist at Rawa, but thought better of the aggression.

Rawa pulled out a device and pressed a number of spots. An Aran-like being appeared in the break room—a confused and unhappy Keeki from the look on his face.

"*unknown location,*
noncontact,
confusion with everything."

Okay, that's definitely our Aran, I thought.

"Yes, Aran, we just found out about your unfortunate abduction. Have you been hurt in any way? Did you receive food and necessities?" asked Major Craig.

"*necessities provided,*
loneliness,
confusion and anger."

"A situation, brought upon by this Similo called Rawa," said Mom, pointing in the alien's direction. "Have a seat, Aran. I'm sure you'll want to hear what Rawa is about to divulge. We certainly do. Mist, perhaps you could get food and drink for Aran, if he requires anything."

Major Craig scowled at Rawa. "You have a lot of explaining to do, so it's time to start. Everyone take seats. Please take notes—I want your impressions."

Rawa joined my mother at her table, and Tyne and I sat down with Aran.

"I may take what sounds like a roundabout way in my explanation. The situation involving my race is complicated," said

Rawa. He took a deep breath. "My beings, the Similo, are the Guardians of this arm of the galaxy."

"This arm of the Milky Way Galaxy?" Cam anticipated my question.

"That is your given name," said Rawa. "We, of course, have another, but that one will suffice."

"Who made *you* our guardians?" I asked. Still irritated, my recent experiences made his words difficult to ignore.

"All will be revealed. Let me speak." Apparently, Rawa didn't appreciate being interrupted.

I shut up—at least, for the moment. I really didn't like his delivery.

Rawa continued, "We have been asked to choose new Guardians."

"Why? What's happened? Who asked you to choose?" I couldn't stop asking questions. Years of practice, however, gave my mother the ability to throw a look my way that made me bite my tongue.

"Rawa, you have a few things to explain," said Major Craig. "Let's start with—why are new guardians needed?" she asked, taking over my questioning.

Rawa hesitated, but then he glanced at my mother and saw the resolve in her eyes. "In the near future, the Similo will leave this galaxy, so we were told to choose new watchers, new guardians."

Interesting. He used the words *told to choose* rather than *asked to choose*. Who watched the watchers?

"How many races were available for your choosing?" asked my mother.

"I cannot say," replied Rawa.

"Cannot or will not?" asked Major Craig. The break room buzzed with conversations.

Rawa declined to answer, and I recognized my mother's growing annoyance. Then she sighed. "How did you decide whom to choose?"

"We tested numerous groups, in various ways. Due to circumstances, we had limited options. That is all I will say."

"Most importantly, what do you mean by *circumstances*?" I asked. No one scolded me for interrupting—the curiosity in the break room flooded my mind.

"Incompatibility," he answered.

Rawa hadn't pounded me down for asking my question, so I decided I'd won a prize today.

I thought about the locations we'd experienced on our expedition. "We haven't found much life on the planets we've investigated. The Similo are poisonous, aren't they? Do they destroy everything they come in contact with?"

We all read the agreement on his face.

"Are you poisonous to us, too?" I asked.

"We are not hazardous to humans or Keeki. However, we do have some negative impact on other races. We did not destroy the planets you visited; life had already disappeared. Please remember that. However, it became clear we had other types of impact on those planets."

I'd suspected as much. "Why did life disappear on these locations?"

"Unknown. Yours to discover," said Rawa.

"What do you mean?" asked Major Craig.

"Earthlings and Keeki have been chosen as the new guardians of this arm of the galaxy."

Silence descended. Even I had a loss of words. My mind raced with all the possibilities Rawa's statement implied.

"Aran and I, as leaders of the humans and Keeki on this expedition, need to understand how your decision was made. Why did you choose our two races? And we need a detailed response," said Major Craig.

"You performed well on all tests you encountered," said Rawa. "Humans and Keeki have an unique relationship—each with their own strengths."

I really didn't like the idea of having been required to perform, but I kept my mouth shut.

"What tests are you referring to?" asked Major Craig.

My mother's stance came across as annoyed, and my relationship led me to believe she was *more* than annoyed.

"You deciphered all the puzzles presented—the pyramids, the plates in various places, and such, and all were very well done. And I must say, the teamwork exhibited amazed us."

"Did you tailor the puzzles based on what you'd uncovered about us?" I asked.

"Yes. I found your activities fascinating," said Rawa. "Quite a bright group."

A little patronizing, I thought. Although if I had god-like powers, I might be too.

"Aside from puzzles, how else did you test us?" asked Major Craig.

"As you now understand, I infiltrated your group disguised as Aran. After I gained knowledge of your relationships, I began my experiments."

Not particularly happy finding out I'd been one of a number of test subjects, my annoyance grew when Rawa said, "I needed to put a human in uncomfortable situations, so I chose Mileena."

As I rose from my seat in protest, Tyne put a hand on my shoulder and gently pressed me down. Probably just as well, as I was about to start spewing words, and no one needed to see me lose control.

"What do you mean?" asked my mother.

"I was the one who made Mile seem awkward." Rawa glanced my way, trying to gauge my reaction, I suspected. He didn't know me very well, so I decided to let the situation play out a bit before having a fit.

My mother arched her eyebrow—Ms. Spock in action. She amused me, and took some of the sting out of Rawa's words. "Please elaborate."

"I gave Mileena a push in the cave; I gave her a nudge down the snow hill; and I interfered in other situations."

I heard uncertainty in Rawa's words, and that surprised me.

"And why did you do that?" asked Mom.

"I wanted to see how the collective reacted to Mileena's predicaments." His head swiveled back and forth between Mom and me.

His words cheered me—I wasn't klutzy!

Tyne leaned over and whispered in my ear. "Kisses soon."

An offer like that I wouldn't say no to.

"Rawa, humans have rules against physical aggression. Do you understand what I'm saying?" asked Major Craig.

"You are saying I overstepped my bounds?" Rawa's body stilled.

Mom nodded. We all understood Rawa's acceptance, after the bowed his head.

Then Rawa said, "You will not like my next statement."

Everyone in the break room focused on the alien. *Now what is he going to admit to?*

"I subjected Mileena and Tyne to further tests," Rawa continued.

"This isn't a revelation. You've already admitted to that," said Major Craig.

"Yes, but these further tests were the final hurdle. If Tyne and Mileena were unsuccessful, sanctions would have been leveled against Earth and Keeki."

My mind exploded. Everything, everyone, our whole existence, depended on Tyne and me?

Tyne grabbed my hand and calmed me a trifle, but not quite enough. I had a mad on.

A hush came over the break room. And Mom took a long time to respond. Finally, she said, "I assume you're telling us Mile and Tyne successfully navigated your testing regime?"

"Yes. Their responses were more than adequate. Although, some of their personal actions eluded me."

Adequate? We were only adequate?

Mom hid a smile. "You do know young people are usually forbidden to be test subjects?"

"I understand. I am willing to undergo any necessary punishment," Rawa responded.

His statement silenced the room. The first conciliatory statement heard from Rawa, confused us. And, I wasn't sure I actually believed his words. With his omnipotent powers, he could do whatever he wanted.

Mom glanced at Tyne and me, and then said, "Perhaps you'd like to discuss your tests, so we get a better idea of Tyne and Mile's experiences."

"I subjected them to a maze, further puzzles, more logic thinking, and finally a physical challenge."

Mom studied Tyne and me. She needed further information since Rawa had become silent.

So I obliged. "He sent the two of us down a river on a raft. You can imagine how well that went," I quipped.

Our expedition members burst into laughter. Then I looked at Tyne and remembered our adventure. Parts of our journey down the river I'd actually enjoyed—although Tyne's opinion may have differed.

Major Craig asked, "So my trusty cadets satisfied your tests?"

"Yes." Rawa added nothing further, but continued to stand before Major Craig's table.

"And now we're to be guardians?" asked my mother.

Rawa made a head motion I believed indicated yes.

"Were there other species considered for this honor?" I asked, as tactfully as I could. Rawa's admissions, regarding my part in the testing, had made me uncomfortable.

"Yes," replied Rawa.

"Who are they?" asked Major Craig.

"Yours to discover." Rawa wouldn't look anyone in the eye. A species trait?

What were we going to do? Not my decision, of course, but my mental question revealed countless opportunities.

"So what happens now?" asked Major Craig. Apparently, we really did think alike.

"You accompany me to my planet for further instructions," said Rawa.

"Instructions about what?" asked my mother. Orders from aliens didn't sit well with Major Craig.

"Your duties as guardians. Humans and Keeki work well together."

"Yes, you keep saying that," said Major Craig. After a moment's silence, she added, "I'm going to have get instructions from my superiors, as I'm sure Aran will from his. We may be forbidden to accompany you until further information is gathered."

"No instructions. The expedition must travel with me," said Rawa. "No choice."

I suspected Rawa had just announced our abduction if we didn't readily accompany him. He'd already shown Tyne and me his capabilities.

My mother understood Rawa's threat. "Not very friendly statements from a guardian—one asking for complete obedience with insufficient information." Mom sighed. "Given your god-like powers, Rawa, I'm sure you can whisk all of us away, never to be seen again." She glared at him. "However, I'm sure you realize that if you want cooperation, you must give us time to adjust. Humans and Keeki are like that. Even a small amount of time is needed, so we can't possibly leave until tomorrow. I must send a message to Earth, and I'm sure Aran will need to inform the Keeki. We need to wait for return messages."

Major White, interrupting a staring match between Mom and Rawa, asked, "What are the coordinates of our new location?"

Rawa hesitated, but eventually dictated the numbers to John.

"We need a day to prepare, Rawa. You may return tomorrow afternoon." Major Craig gave him his walking papers, and I tried not to cheer.

Surprising me, he disappeared without another word. Rawa had apparently decided to respect our idiosyncrasies.

Was I being naïve? Were reinforcements on the way?

Major Craig studied her expedition crew. "I don't like our situation, but we need to wait to hear what Earth and Keeki have to say. Take the rest of the day off. Go outside and get some exercise. But also batten down the hatches—complete any outstanding reports, solve puzzles, and such. Our future is uncertain; we need to be prepared."

"But…"

Major Craig interrupted my one word with a strong glance. "You all know as much as I do. Prepare yourselves for any eventuality. Relaxation is appropriate, but not an easy task given our uncertain futures. Now I must leave. I have urgent messages to send."

Sylone and Aran left the break room, accompanied by John. An oasis of silence remained.

Finding a grip on our situation eluded me, so I decided satisfying hunger was next on my agenda. Time had flown, and it was well past lunch time. Tyne joined me, but our conversation fizzled. I still reeled from the shock of our testing and Rawa's revelations, and I suspected Tyne had his own similar issues.

Eventually, my thought processes calmed, so I finished and cleaned up my lunch residue. By this time, Aran, Mom, and John had returned to the break room.

While my mind still rumbled around today's unsettling revelations, Tyne rose and went over and spoke with Sylone and Aran. Then the three of them left.

Now what's that all about?

Feeling abandoned by my favorite people, I grabbed my pack and went outside.

I wandered about Wyre, without a particular purpose in mind. Of course, our short sojourn hadn't revealed enough information for me to focus on any destination. After walking a short distance, I decided the flat rock I spied would make a fine place to stop and think.

So that's what I did. My mind wandered over the past few days' captivity and then on to Rawa's pronouncements. What a tangled mess we'd landed in.

An arm snaked around my waist interrupting my ruminations—Tyne had found me.

We kissed, and then I asked, "Where have you been? Why did you go with my mother and Aran?"

Tyne knew about my relationship to Major Craig, I suspected. He'd mentioned earlier we had the same smell, which had kind of freaked me out, at the time.

"*both leaders,*
discussion,
transfer of authority."

I shook my head. I had no idea what his words meant. "Tyne, try again. I don't know what you're trying to say."

"*transferring allegiance,*
joining,
Earth Sciences Force."

This time, his words gave me great hope. "Really? You're going to be a cadet with ESF? I'm so happy!" After I recognized the truth in his eyes, I hugged Tyne for the longest time. Of course, our hugging escalated.

Finally, I took a deep breath and asked, a little belatedly, "Both Major Craig and Aran agreed to this transfer?" My mother was a possibility, but Aran seemed a long shot. Of course, Rawa's actions had tarnished my perception of Aran.

"*parents deceased,*
transfer,
remain with Mileena."

I gave him a kiss. "Both Mom and Aran agreed right away?" He really hadn't answered my question yet.

"*decision against,*
refuse,

remain on Wyre."

"So you gave them no choice? You would have stayed on Wyre no matter what? And they agreed?"

Tyne smiled. "Together."

He had me with his words. Much to my surprise, I realized I would've stayed behind on this planet with Tyne—practical objections aside, of course.

Thankfully, we wouldn't need to make that decision.

I gave Tyne a kiss, and asked, "Shall we return to *Skyfall*? I'm getting hungry. Must be approaching dinner time."

Tyne grabbed my hand, and we returned to the ship, in harmony. We'd be together, no matter what happened.

After we joined Squid and Mist, in the break room, something made me study the two of them. Their human and Keeki smiles gave everything away.

"Squid, are you…" I asked.

"Mile, I know you're my friend. Don't ask," he interrupted.

My mouth hung open for the longest time, but eventually I muttered, "How about a nonogram tournament tonight? Who knows when we'll have another chance?"

"How difficult should we make the tournament, and who has a nonogram we could try?" asked Squid.

A couple of good questions. Cam dined at another table, but I got his attention. "Are you up for a nonogram tournament?"

"Sorry, no. I have a lab full of samples to test."

I laughed. "Yes, we've certainly been filling up your available space. Do you have any nonograms we could work on? I know you love them."

Cam smiled. "Actually, I do. A great one. Who's all in?" He counted hands and said, "Give me two minutes and I'll send my nonogram to the printer." Cam glanced around the room. "Have a great time. I wish I could join you."

Shortly, the printer started chugging out paper, and our tournament had begun.

Cam, of course, had sent us a large and complicated nonogram, but no one complained. The evening whiled away, and the general consensus was that our competition was the perfect way to end our sojourn on Wyre. Even Aran, Major Craig, and Major White joined us in our endeavors.

Eventually, we declared Squid the victor and Major Craig broke out the alcohol and let everyone have their favorite.

"It's been a long and stressful day," she said. "So I'm glad everyone is continuing to bond."

I assumed she meant over puzzles.

"Have an early night. I should be able to relay Earth's responses at breakfast." Mom and John left, and Aran wasn't far behind.

"Sort of a good day?" I asked Tyne, when we were alone.

"*situation stressful,*
excellent,
remaining with you."

Words that needed no further explanation. "Tyne, it's time for me to retire. Join me?"

He rubbed my ear, and grabbed my hand.

Chapter Twenty-Nine

home government
excited
races to meet

The next morning, Tyne and I entered the break room together. Our entrance did not go unnoticed, but no one commented loud enough to reach my ears. Of course, I probably imagined the whispers.

We joined Squid and Mist at their table. The only ones missing were Mom and John, but they soon arrived and settled at Aran's table. We gave them a few moments to obtain fuel for our soon-to-be-stressful day.

After a reasonably short time, Mom stood and the break room occupants went silent.

"Much to my disbelief, and Aran's surprise, both Earth and Keeki have responded to our messages."

Then she stopped talking.

Why isn't she saying anything? Are their responses so bad?

After a tense moment, Cam said, "If you don't tell us what they said—and in a timely manner—I'm going to stop testing, in a timely manner."

Cam did know how to make us laugh.

Major Craig responded in the same way. "Of course, Cam, but only because you asked so nicely."

Laughter broke out. Between the two of them, they'd released a majority of the tension in the break room. Well, at least amongst the humans.

Mom started to speak and our attention returned to her. "Earth has decided we have no choice but to follow Rawa. Being *Guardians of the Galaxy*, one arm of it at least, intrigued them. This is a good thing, I believe." Mom studied the room. "Since we have the coordinates of Rawa's world, Earth knows where we're going, so they've decided to send a number of ships to rendezvous with us. The ships will be carrying diplomats, and who knows what else."

"More food, more alcohol," quipped someone behind me.

Mom laughed and studied the expedition members. A serious look appeared on her face. "If anyone doesn't like our new situation then, when our human ships arrive at Rawa's planet, you'll be free to return to Earth. No questions asked."

Sylone waited out the murmuring. "Unfortunately, I see no way to return anyone home anytime sooner than that."

Although I suspected Rawa could probably transport anyone anywhere, I kept my counsel and looked at the humans in the break room. No confusion or major anxiety was evident to me.

Apparently, Major Craig came to the same conclusion because she said, "Aran has some words for the Keeki."

The Keeki leader stood.

"*home government,*
excited,
races to meet."

Okay, so the Keeki wanted to meet new races, but did they want to be guardians?

Then Aran added,

"*friendships earned,*
Keeki,
meeting Similo forces."

So Keeki from their home world were also going to rendezvous at Rawa's planet. If my interpretation was correct, it should be an interesting experience for everyone involved.

"In case anyone's confused about our explanations, this expedition will be travelling to Rawa's home. We're part of an expedition I'd never imagined," said Major Craig.

Many conversations broke out around the break room. Then Rawa appeared, much to everyone's surprise.

"I wasn't expecting you until this afternoon," said my mother. "Have you been listening to our conversations?"

"Yes, of course. For more reasons than you could imagine."

"So what's next?" she asked, with resignation in her voice.

"Everyone, please sit down," said Rawa.

"Why? When are we going to your home world?" asked Major Craig.

"In about one second," said Rawa. "It really is much easier if you are seated."

TO BE CONTINUED

A word about the author…

After accumulating books on writing for many years, Roxanne kicked thirty years of procrastination out the door in 2011, and started writing.

Roxanne can be reached at hyperlight@hyperwarp.com.

Publications (Novels):

- Revolutions
- Sacred Trust
- Alien Innkeeper
- Kaiku
- An Alien Perspective

Made in the USA
Charleston, SC
27 February 2017